BAHIR

SURVIVING THE WORLD OUTSIDE

Monisha K Gumber

authorHOUSE®

AuthorHouse™
1663 Liberty Drive
Bloomington, IN 47403
www.authorhouse.com
Phone: 1 (800) 839-8640

This is a work of fiction. All of the characters, names, incidents,
organizations, and dialogue in this novel are either the products
of the author's imagination or are used fictitiously.

Published by AuthorHouse 10/25/2018

ISBN: 978-1-5462-6499-6 (sc)
ISBN: 978-1-5462-6498-9 (hc)
ISBN: 978-1-5462-6497-2 (e)

Library of Congress Control Number: 2018912615

Print information available on the last page.

This book is printed on acid-free paper.

DEDICATION:

To my very strong and beautiful sisters Mona and Rashmi

FOREWORD

I badly need a haircut. That's what I always say to myself whenever I look in the mirror and see a face that's getting softer and a jawline that's slowly disappearing. I then look at the big picture (!)– despite the random hours spent on the treadmill and daily twenty minutes of Pranayama, I am nowhere near my goal of being able to wear that shimmering black saree with a backless blouse on my anniversary. Growing up is not fun once you hit forty. Because after that it's like you can never be in your thirties again. For the last few years I don't think I have ever gone to bed without planning my diet and exercise routine. Usually it doesn't last more than a day. But recently, I realized I was counting on these salons to restore my youth and beauty. A pedicure and eyebrows usually does the trick. But nothing can beat a new hairstyle for lifting your spirits.

Well, this is just one of those days, as mostly I don't really care. But today I do, so let me try to do something dramatic for a change. Tonight Sunny is coming home after a week of those boring, never-ending board meetings; so let me take out that shocking-pink lingerie that's been lying in my cupboard for ages. So, with a new hairstyle and some red lipstick, I will try making him excited in bed again. I hope this time I don't fail. I also hope that the lingerie still fits.

Before you get even more interested to find out what happened that night, I have a confession to make. This is not my story. It's actually the story of the hairstylist I went to for that dramatic look. But something even more dramatic happened. This book.

'Madam – did you recognize me? It's me – Sawera.'

I turn around and see a stunning face with the same small nose and glossed, bee-stung lips. And those enigmatic eyes – those shiny black

Arabian pearls – still reflect her grey and humid past, adding to the mystery. Oh, why is God so generous with some women?

We hug and I feel her delicious scent. And the same old pang of envy returns. Nothing personal. Just something a woman feels when she sees someone more beautiful. Even more so, as the small nose has a diamond on it now.

'Sawera! What are you doing here? I thought you had left the country!' I exclaimed.

'Madam, I did, but came back. You know, one can never leave Bahrain.' She smiled.

Yes, I knew. Like those thousands of expatriates, we come, fall in love with this place; after a few years realize we miss home and leave for good. But that 'good' doesn't last longer than a year or two as we come back again. Bahrain. The land of a million palm trees and even more smiles. A small island with a big heart.

'Yes, I know . . . I didn't know you worked here. Such a swanky place,' I said wonderingly.

'Actually, madam, it's my own. Remember, I used to tell you about my dream. *Alhamdulillah*, it finally happened. Reshma Salon and Spa,' she said, with a childlike twinkle in those eyes.

'Wonderful, Sawera, I am so proud of you. I came for a haircut but that can wait. Tell me everything, do you still do massage? We could talk there,' I suggested.

'Usually I don't, but for my old customers like you, madam, I will do anything,' she assured me.

I knew she meant it. She is the same Sawera who used to go from house to house, threading, waxing and massaging her way to support her four children in Pakistan. Beautiful from inside, too. Despite having lived such an ugly life. But I needed to know everything. From the very start. Especially now that she had finally made it. And what could be a better place to talk than a spa?

SAUDI ARABIA

A CHILLY NIGHT IN NOVEMBER, 1978:

LAKKAR MANDI VILLAGE, MULTAN DISTRICT, PAKISTAN

*'M*ubarak, Reshma, your prayers have been answered. You have become a mother.'

Ammi was too stunned to react but her hands automatically went up towards the holy skies to thank the *Ar-Rahman, Ar-Rahim,* her Allah who had bestowed this title on her. My Ammi had finally become one, when I was born.

In the other room of our dilapidated house, lay Khala on the floor, supervised by Dai-ma and her self-proclaimed assistant, a haggard old lady from the neighbourhood. I am told that it was a very long and difficult labour, spread over twelve hours through the coldest night of the season. When I was born I was still in the shell of the caul – maybe it was my way of telling the world that I would always need protection; but nature is cruel. My slippery cover was torn apart when I was pulled out and handed over to my Ammi, who had been waiting for my arrival for the last ten years. No cleaning up. No bath. Given away. In raw flesh and blood.

Sixth-born to my Khala but Abbu-Ammi's first daughter. Their *laddo, khuda ki niyamat* – their baby – midnight's child named Sawera – the first irony of my life. It was a pact between my Khala, the one who gave birth to me, and my Ammi, who brought me up, that I would be handed over as soon as I was born. Ammi and Abbu had been desperately trying to have a child for a decade and after three miscarriages and hundreds of visits to the *pir* babas, Ammi begged my Khala to bail her out, else Abbu would have remarried a potentially more fertile girl from the village. We were all poor but still extravagant when it came to children. Did not mind having a lot or even giving away one or two to the needy. Especially when the needy one happened to be your sister. Khala was very kind, but I am not sure if she was fair.

My birth gave my Ammi a new confidence. Like all women of our community, her sense of worth came from how her mother-in-law treated her, which came from how many children she could bear. Married off at just fifteen to a widower cousin double her age, her only hope was getting pregnant as soon as possible. Pure like a white dove, with a voluptuous bosom and swaying hips, as inviting as moist farming soil, it came as a rude shock when she failed in her foremost duty as a woman. It did not matter if she was the most beautiful woman in the village. It did not matter that her husband loved her. The fact that she was unable to bear children degraded her to a non-existent being. Her old mother-in-law was already looking for a second wife for her son. My birth saved my Ammi. And not just once.

I wasn't considered a lucky charm for nothing. Just nine months later, Ammi became a mother again. This time for real. Omar came into this world, stilling the wagging tongues of our relatives once and for all. Sometimes I wonder if Ammi and Abbu made out the same night I came into this world, and conceived their first born. My twin brother – or almost.

Abba used to work as a carpenter for a small furniture shop in Muneerabad. Like all ambitious young men, he too had a dream of going *bahir*. He was sick of seeing his delicate wife slogging in poverty amidst the harsh tirades of his cruel mother. It was time to make some decisions. I think the birth of his son made him believe enough in himself again to venture into new territory. He was jealous of his cousins, returning from the Gulf with bags full of imported toys and perfumes. Some of them even brought gold bangles. He heard fascinating stories of skyscrapers, air-conditioned cars and belly-dancers. He now wanted to live that life. If not, he would be content with a new motorcycle and perhaps a small house of his own. But even for such bare necessities he had to get out of these accursed lanes of his village.

He sold off his wife's gold chain, his land and his two goats to accumulate enough money for an agent. At first, the women of the house were very hesitant to send him off but the lure of a good life was enough to bid him goodbye. They chose to rubbish the somewhat different story of another cousin who returned from a Gulf country after ten years with nothing but a frail body and an empty spirit. The poor man was robbed of his belongings as soon as he landed there and was made to work in the excoriating Middle-East summers as a construction worker, sometimes twelve hours at a stretch, even during Ramzaan. When he tried running away, he was kept practically a prisoner for three years until the government declared amnesty and some lucky illegal immigrants were allowed to return to their homelands.

When I was born, the Dai-ma had warned Khala against giving me up as she claimed to have a sixth sense that it was going to get very complicated. But the deal was done. And things had actually started to look better for my adoptive family. Abbu went off to Saudi and his life took the turn he was waiting for. His sponsor owned a chain of furniture shops in Riyadh and instantly took a liking for this pleasing new worker from Pakistan with honest eyes and willingness to work like a donkey. The sponsor (known as an *arbab* in the Gulf), recently cheated by his own brother and business partner, was desperate for someone he could depend on. He took my Abbu under his wing. Slowly, Abbu learnt to fly on his own. He was not only a very skilled craftsman, but a man who could be trusted blindly. Within five years Abbu rose through the ranks and earned a supervisor's position in his *arbab's* factory. All these years, we were in our village waiting for the day Abbu would come home to take his family away from these dusty, run-down, dark streets of Lakkar Mandi.

I realize now that those early so-called dark years were probably the best part of my life. Because that's when I was truly loved and taken care of. Ammi attributed her better fortune to me and never let me go out of her sight. Omar and I played all the time and had no dearth of toys or milk, much to the envy of our neighbours. We were both spoilt to the core but I was her favourite. Another advantage for Ammi was that Dadi died and finally her status in the family was sealed. She was no more answerable to anyone about how to run her house or bring up her children, loving the independence and the privilege of doing everything by herself without having to ask Abbu or Dadi. Still, I think she missed him. I was too young to understand everything but I do know that Adil Chacha used to visit our house a lot and never brought his wife with him. I do know that he spent a lot of time behind closed doors with my Ammi but God forgive me if I am just being over-imaginative.

The fateful day came and Abbu came back with the good news that his *arbab* had agreed to process a family visa and now all the papers were through. All these years we had hardly had any contact with Khala's family as they never wanted me to find out the truth about my adoption. Khala cut herself off from me completely, as Ammi, despite her delicate exterior, was a very strong woman indeed. She forbade anyone to see me as she was too afraid of letting go of her lucky mascot. So, leaving Pakistan was going to work. I wonder – in her excitement of going abroad, did she ever think about Adil Chacha?

FEBRUARY 1985:

Riyadh, Kingdom of Saudi Arabia

Back in those days, Indian films were our only link to a civilized world of wide roads, tall buildings and sensual women without burqas. I still remember our flight from Peshawar airport to Riyadh. We, who had never even been to the local bus stand, found ourselves in a real aeroplane with these lovely made-up women serving us juice. Oh, what a life was going to begin. Omar was scared of the sudden change of events but I could not contain my excitement. I was born for this. It didn't matter that all the women outside the plane, when we landed, were covered from head to toe.

Bahir. Foreign. Abroad. I knew that whatever it was, life was going to change.

Abbu brought us to his flat on the top floor of a four-storey building. We went up in a tiny room, which we were later told was called a lift. At the press of a button we could go from the ground to the sky. The flat we moved into had one small hall, a bedroom, a kitchen and a bathroom with a western-style toilet. Oh, so this is how the rich live. Ammi hardly spoke; it was going to take her a long time to get used to the comforts of foreign life.

Even at that young age, I could sense the simmering attraction between Abbu and Ammi. In our culture, parents don't really try getting physically close in front of their children but in our home I saw them shamelessly kissing at least three to four times.

So, in less than a year of our moving to Saudi, little Rashid came into this world. As I said, life was going to change.

I was probably seven or eight at that time. Abbu left me with Omar to attend to Ammi's delivery. He told me to take charge and not get worried if he got late. He locked the main door and went off, leaving two small children to look after each other. We were anyway not allowed to ever visit our American neighbours as he did not want any western influence on his vulnerable family.

I have no one but Ammi to blame for what happened next. Had she not pampered me so much, I would have never been insane enough to do this. When evening fell, Omar and I started getting really restless. I had been told to take charge but Omar's nervousness was beginning to have an effect on me. In Lakkar Mandi we were used to living without electricity but when the lights went off that night, we both started wailing with fright. Too afraid to face those imaginary djinns and in a desperate attempt to save my brother, I opened the window of our hall and started calling out for help. When no one seemed to hear me, I decided to go down the drainpipe that ran down the wall outside and get someone to enter the building from the front gate and unlock the main door of our flat. I was too young to understand the implications of my stupidity. I wish I had not seen that Superman movie on TV as the next moment I found myself hanging from the railings of the window. I knew that I was dead – because even if I survived, Abbu would kill me.

I have no idea how long I hung on to the railings but when I looked down, I could see that people had started to gather round and commotion was slowly building up. I just remember crying a lot till I heard a deep calm voice, which said, 'Let go.' I did and landed straight into the arms of an Arab in a pure-white *thobe* – the kind you see in detergent commercials. The moment I saw his face, I fainted.

When I opened my eyes, I was still groggy as I had no idea if I was still alive. Maybe heaven looked like my own house. I saw Abbu and Omar standing next to me. They told me that Ammi had delivered and was coming home the next day.

Even now, this incident is always narrated in all family gatherings since then, much to my embarrassment. Abbu tried finding out about that Arab in white, but no one had an idea who he was and where he had come from. I am sure he was my *farishta*, a guardian angel who has made a few more appearances in my life since then.

And I would need a *farishta* – repeatedly. Because, from that day onward, I actually became helpless. Little Rashid's birth changed a lot of things for me. Ammi got busy with taking care of him and Abbu was always away at work. Omar had started growing up into a rowdy bastard who did not need his sister any more as he had his own brother for a toy. Someone he could push around and take advantage of. Ammi started paying more attention to her sons and began referring to Omar as the man of the house. I could sense the whole family teaming up against me and I was slowly becoming their soft target. I was always blamed if a toy got broken, if the milk got spilled, if the rice got burnt or if Ammi had one of her regular headaches. Her boys were always the innocent victims of this conniving devil sister of theirs – me. All these years, Abbu and Ammi had never raised a hand on me, so it felt like a thunderbolt when I got hit for the first time. I still do not remember why but, like I said, when she saw Omar beating up Rashid, she decided to thrash me for just watching instead of mediating like a responsible big sister. I forgave her then as I thought she loved me too much to do it deliberately. Maybe she was just in a bad mood.

The headaches turned into full-fledged migraine attacks and the bad mood turned into depression. I think Ammi was torn between the tough but exciting village life and the comfortable but boring loneliness this city had given her.

1990:

AL KHOBAR, KINGDOM OF SAUDI ARABIA

Abbu was like all men from the subcontinent – hard-working, dependable and *jugadu*. And thanks to me, he had started getting luckier than most. His luck was probably rubbing off on to his sponsor too, as the furniture business was growing and they decided to expand into other cities. Abbu was rewarded with a whole new showroom in a whole new city. When we got to know about it, our joy knew no bounds. Being diehard optimists we were fully prepared for happier times.

With an extra bedroom, a company car (all right, so it was an old pick-up) and a part-time maid, we knew that Abbu had made it big in life. Ammi too came out of her depressive cocoon and decided to give her life a chance. She realized that it was easier to fight boredom than to face poverty. Abbu had always been a timid God-fearing family man but Ammi was a free bird. Despite Abbu's disapproval, she started mingling with other ladies in our building. Guests started visiting and the family started forming a social circle. After all, there has never been a shortage of Pakistanis in Saudi. Women always have to be in *abayas,* especially in public places, but Ammi loved showing off her new chiffon sarees in private gatherings. Ammi now possessed her own gold bangles.

In Riyadh, we used to go to a run-down government school next to our house but here, I joined Global Urdu School for Girls. After all, Ammi had to match up to the status of her new-found friends.

From a petite girl with lots of facial hair, I was changing into a beautiful young thing with my own pair of glasses and my own pair of boobs. I would spend hours in the bathroom exploring the changes my body was bringing. It was exhilarating and very scary too. The girls in my class loved discussing periods, bras and boys. Somehow, I have always had the knack of attracting trouble, so most of my friends were the so-called fast girls from rich families. This is when we all discovered this sticky magical potion that ripped off the unwanted hair on legs, arms and even face with a few painful strokes! Yes. It's called waxing and it's totally worth it.

Ammi had never prepared me for this transition but I think children have their own sources – mostly each other. So if parents think they are protecting their kids by not discussing the changes puberty brings, they are mistaken. Unfortunately, children discover everything on their own and sometimes it's not pretty. And certainly not reliable.

When I got my periods, instead of feeling gross like most of my friends, I got turned on thinking that now I could be a mother and have my own babies, my own husband and my own house. I am one of those stupid girls who have always wanted to get married. If Ammi had talked to me even once about it, I would have not been so naïve. Or, maybe, too smart for my own good.

Once I was invited to a birthday party by the most popular girl in my class, who came from a well-known family. Actually everyone was and I did not want to be an outcast by not going. I knew my Ammi would refuse but I begged and begged. I even pleaded with the birthday girl's mother to personally call up my Ammi and ask her to let me go. Aunty assured her that there would be no male guests. Ammi reluctantly gave in as she did not want others to feel that we came from such a conservative background. Still, I had to go in my *abaya* and *hijab*.

Oh, what a party it was! The girls looked like little Bollywood starlets in their sleeveless dresses. Ammi had strictly warned me not to remove my coverings but when I saw the girls dancing away to *bhangra* beats, I got carried away and joined in too, without my 'protection'. Maybe I deserved this for not listening to Ammi as the next moment I twisted my ankle and went crashing down to the floor. It was so bad that I could not walk properly. When Ammi saw me limping in that night, she accused me of 'doing it all' with someone I probably met in that modern girl's party! I was called a *haramzadi* just because I got up to dance. She beat me up so much that I carried the bruises for weeks. My real bruises took an even longer time to heal. The bruises to my soul.

Though I came to know the truth about my adoption a long time later, that night I understood. Ammi did not love me any more. I was bullied by Omar, teased by Rashid and completely ignored by Abbu. I badly needed to be loved and accepted. By anyone and anywhere.

Enter: Victor Uncle. Our new neighbour and Abbu's old acquaintance from Riyadh. With a Masters in English from one of the best universities in India. Or so he claimed. Abbu's happiness knew no bounds when Uncle volunteered to give tuitions to his children and that too for free. Indians were not as bad as we thought. When I saw him for the first time, I knew he was the one. A tall, dark and educated South Indian with a heavy accent and well-oiled black hair. He was probably Abbu's age or even older but this man knew how to take care of himself. Always dressed immaculately in chequered shirts and formal pants, a completely different picture from my balding Abbu, with a growing belly, in old Pathani suits.

He worked as a salesman in a car showroom and used to get a long lunch break. After his meal, he would do his social service of teaching children like us who were not so good at English. Both Omar and I used to look forward to the visits of this charming man who would never come empty-handed. We felt like real human beings and not just his friends' children who could be bought easily with chocolates. He did a little more.

When he asked me about my 'likes and dislikes', it was as though I was important enough to even have a like or a dislike, whatever that meant. Imagine how I must have felt when he went further and deeper and spoke about my 'strengths and weaknesses'! I realized much later in life that these are the hot topics with Indians – they analyze, argue and have an opinion about everything! And they make their children prepare for job interviews earlier than the rest of the world. Anyway, coming back to my love story, then I was a just a young school girl who could not help feeling attracted to this dark-skinned *angrez* and started dreaming about the time when we could be alone without having Omar in the same room. But I was not the only one who felt this way. Once I caught Uncle staring at me and then he sent Omar off to fetch a glass of water for him. Ammi was sound asleep in the other room. And then it happened. My first kiss. When his lips touched mine, I felt this was the moment I had been longing for, all my life. So this was love. I did not know how to respond but neither did I resist.

Usually I dreaded coming home from school to face Ammi's never-ending bickering but now I couldn't wait for the last bell to ring so that I could rush back home and wait for my teacher. He, too, got a little bolder and started asking Omar to go to another room to write an essay in two hundred words. You know how long that can take for a child whose English is poor. So our kissing sessions turned longer too. Oh, how wonderful it was! Except that the usual taste of *sambar* on his lips was beginning to repel me a little.

Yet again, I had not realized that I was not the only one who felt like this. Once, our school finished half an hour earlier than usual. This was the only game Omar and I played: whenever we came back from school, he would take the steps and I would take the lift to race to the top. Mostly he won and today once again I lost. Despite winning.

When I banged open the main door, I saw my own Victor Uncle kissing Ammi, exactly the way he used to kiss me. Even his hands were doing their own tricks inside Ammi's blouse, something he had not attempted on me till now. And Ammi surely knew how to respond. Much better than me.

Have you ever heard of a child getting beaten up for coming home from school earlier than usual?

English chapter closed. Else my story would have had some more impressive and complicated words.

FEBRUARY 1992:

KARACHI, PAKISTAN

This was my first visit to Pakistan in so many years. My Khala's eldest daughter Fatima was getting married to a 'government servant', an achievement in itself. Despite the expenses on air tickets, new clothes and gifts, we went, as this was an opportunity for my Ammi to show off her wealth. Compared to regular Saudis we were still not rich but for our extended family in Pakistan, we were nothing less than royalty and were treated the same way too.

Karachi. Located on the Arabian Sea coastline, also known as *Uroos ul Bilaad* or the Bride of the Cities. I never expected Pakistan to be this colourful and modern. The distinctive buildings, structures and monuments were a treat for the eyes. I had not seen such radical architecture even in Saudi. I think I fell in love with its lights, its bazaars, its beaches and its people.

Now I could relate to the excitement of my classmates when they would recount their travel adventures. Most visited their home country at least once a year but some of them had even been to America and Europe. But for me, this was my first vacation ever and probably the best one I have had in my life.

Because this is when I got some real attention. Especially during the various ceremonies, when I could sense my relatives whispering things about me. Something was going on. Was I so beautiful that they were always talking about me?

I found out what the fuss was all about during the *Rasm-e-henna* night. Khala, who was behaving like an emotional wreck, watching her eldest one getting married, could not help shedding a tear or two whenever we came face to face. Though I was looking for love, her hugs, wet kisses and countless blessings were beginning to irritate me.

So here is when I learnt about the conspiracy about my birth. That Khala gave birth to me and Ammi just adopted me as she had no children of her own. Here is when I totally understood why Ammi's behaviour had changed when she had her own children. I still have a picture-perfect memory of that fateful evening when Fatima Apa, dressed in traditional yellow with minimal makeup on her face and intricate *mehendi* on her palms, told me everything. I think the bride was jealous that it was me who had become the centre of attraction instead of her. So she took it out on me. But how wrong she was. Because from this moment onwards, I was mentally free. I did not belong anywhere and had no real family of my own. I was a sham. Was I hurt? Yes, I cried for hours together because that was how I was expected to react. But did I really feel sad? Maybe not.

All the days thereafter, I spent with my real brothers and sisters. We played, bonded, gossiped and went sight-seeing. They took me to some famous tourist attractions like the Mohatta Palace, National Museum and Hill Park. I was like a curious foreigner in my own country.

Now that all was out in the open, Khala could now start behaving normally with me. She talked a lot to me and prepared my favourite *halwa-puri* almost every day. It was a dream come true. Ammi, Omar and Rashid had formed their own rival group and pretended I did not exist at all. What was I supposed to feel? Where would I be living from now on? Would Khala still send me off to Saudi into the hands of an indifferent family? Did Ammi really not love me? Could I stay back if I wanted to?

But a deal is a deal. Nobody asked me how I felt and what I wanted and now I am glad it happened that way as I was too young to know what was good for me. Honestly, even after so many years, I still suffer from the same problem.

A MONTH LATER:

BACK IN AL KHOBAR

We were all back in Saudi, and now it was time for revenge. Earlier I used to merely curse her in my mind whenever she used to beat me. Now I stopped feeling guilty about it. I could now stand up to Omar and myself turned into a bully for little Rashid. Whenever she raised her hand or her voice at me, I would take out my anger and frustration on my younger brother. Slowly I started enjoying it and Ammi had no choice but to give up physically torturing me. Her bickering was turning into sheer contempt. Slowly she became absolutely indifferent. It stopped making any difference if I had food or not, if I did my homework or not or if I went to school or not. I was completely on my own. For some time, I liked the way things were turning out for me but slowly I started missing Ammi's scoldings. Maybe I was happier being an abused daughter instead of a stranger in my own home.

I had to take some serious steps to get her attention once again. Did I say something about being mentally free?

I like to think myself as fairly intelligent despite being not so good in studies. Now that I was in class X and had Board exams, my life was very difficult – both at home and at school. But sometimes fun, too. As I said, my group of friends was the spoilt girls from so-called liberal families. In Saudi, it is compulsory for girls to be covered from head to toe, usually in the same black cloak called *abaya*, but some of them actually wore skirts to private parties. They had these pajama nights where they watched English films and discussed boys. Particularly since the birthday party debacle, I was not allowed to mingle with them outside school but on the pretext of exam preparation, I could managed to go to my best friend Farah's house once.

Her mother was a doctor, one of the few fields where women were allowed to work. It was 14 August – the Pakistani Independence Day – so our school was off but her parents were away at work. She called me to her house along with a few other girls. When Abbu dropped me there he warned me to behave and avoid being too close with this girl who lived in a big house and was obviously spoilt. I had to just study, mind my own business and be ready when Abbu came in the evening to pick me up. Because he was not going to wait even for a minute outside the gate.

When I went inside I could not believe my eyes. The usually reserved Farah was dressed in all black – not that cloak but a lacy black dress over sheer leggings. I still remember how awkward I felt looking at my simple garb while Farah had plastic accessories and a plastic pout constantly stuck on her heavily made-up face. There were three other girls from my class who were also trying really hard to look sexy for their boyfriends. Yes. For the first time I had a close look at boys other than that villainous Omar and that weakling Rashid. Handsome, rich boys just like the college students who ride bikes in Bollywood films. There was rap music and free-flowing Coke. They were cozying up in pairs except one guy who kept staring at me. Farah dragged me along to introduce me to him as his date. I didn't know what she meant but it made me blush. He held my hand firmly and took me to another room. I was just too willing to comply and couldn't wait for things to move forward. And what guts he had – without saying a word, he took my face in his hands and planted a wet kiss on my quivering lips. My first boyfriend – but what was his name again? Anyway, Happy Independence Day, Sawera!

After that I used the exam excuse often and started going for more such parties but unfortunately I never met him again. He was Farah's cousin visiting from the UK and went back to his life. I was too shy to inquire about him and also I did not want any of my friends to think that I was no longer available for new hook-ups. I knew it was just a matter of time before I got noticed again and perhaps it could lead to more. But I wasn't just longing for a few kisses here and there. I wanted to have a real relationship. I so desperately wanted fall in love that it just did not matter with whom.

Farah's boyfriend Mahmood used to study in the boys' wing just adjacent to our school. Yes, we were in an extremely conservative society but love always finds its ways. Girls and boys used to pass on notes to each other through their younger siblings. The messengers would get paid with chocolates but the more enterprising ones demanded cash and cigarettes too. Couples used to meet in secluded parks, on the Corniche, in empty parking lots, in vacant 'haunted' buildings. Now when I think about it, I shudder to think the risks we were ready to take at that age. The hormones were raging and the urge to be with the opposite sex was driving us all crazy. I think that's what happens when you grow up in such a strict environment – so we were all rebels with this worthy cause of finding true love – with the first one who came along.

Along came Tahir, Mahmood's classmate. Fresh from Pakistan and desperately trying to fit in, when he came to know about this beautiful single girl with big eyes and the biggest boobs in the school, he begged Mahmood and Farah to help him out with her. Of course, I had no choice but to say yes to his proposal that came in a letter. He claimed to love me and would die if I didn't say yes. I did, without even having met him once.

The letters continued from my side too. I poured out my deepest feelings to this stranger. I wrote about my cruel family who would never let me do anything. I wrote about loneliness, about my painful life and how much I needed him to love me and take me away from my troubles. Obviously I wrote about the day we would meet, hold hands, kiss and even have wild sex, whatever it meant. All this to a shy sixteen-year-old school boy who had probably never touched or even seen a girl properly! Imagine what this eroticism would have done to him. Imagine what would happen if we actually met.

We never did. As I was stupid enough to get caught writing a love letter – that too in Maths period. Feeling like a sacrificial goat, I was dragged by my hair to the Principal's office. I kept howling and pleading with them not to inform my parents as they would kill me. Maybe it was better that I died.

But they did something even worse. They pulled me out of school.

I was to stay only at home and cut off all ties with all bad company like my best friend Farah and my boyfriend Tahir whom I hadn't even met. No more books and no more tuitions. Sawera. Not even a Matric pass. Sometimes I wonder how far I could have really got academically anyway, the way I was.

Sitting at home with nothing much to do, the next few months, whenever I was alone and unsupervised, my favorite pastime was to invade my Ammi's cupboard and try out her sarees and makeup. I would turn on the radio and dance with abandon, with nothing but a towel on. I would sway my hips and shake my breasts like those item girls. Oh what crazy adventures I had. Being left alone sure is the sexiest feeling in the world. Did I say it would have been better that I had died?

More months passed. I was sixteen going on seventeen and looking for excitement in my monotonous life. During one such day when my Ammi was out, busy socializing with other housewives in the building, I happened to find this video cassette wrapped in one of her petticoats. I guessed it was something we children were not allowed to touch. But who could stop this girl on a mission? Heavens. I could not believe that it was really happening. So this is what happens between grown men and women. I saw the whole act of the wild sex I had heard so much about from the girls in my school. So this is how one loves.

Since then this was all I thought about. I was probably going mad and Ammi started sensing it too. She dragged me along, whether it was a trip to the market or those boring kitty parties. She did not realize that it wasn't going to work. During one such event, I saw him. Deepak, Renu Aunty's brother. I had accompanied Ammi to their house for some function. When I went to the kitchen to get some water, he followed me and tried making small talk. I learnt that he had just moved to Saudi after his graduation from Delhi. He was going to start working in an oil company as a technician. I took a good look at him and discovered a soft face with beautiful features. Probably he plucked his eyebrows and used Fair and Lovely. His mannerisms were too ladylike and he had a repulsively feminine voice. But I was still drawn towards his kindness. He asked about my life and genuinely shed a couple of tears when I told him I was not allowed to go to school.

You know I always had this thing for Indians.

Those days it was not easy for lovers like us, with no mobile phones or internet, it took an inordinate amount of planning and coordination to arrange a meeting. But it's not for nothing that Pakistanis and Indians do so well in the whole world. We have our ways. Particularly Indians.

Somehow, he got hold of our landline number and started trying his luck. A couple of times Abbu picked up but then Deepak would disconnect or pretend to have dialled a wrong number. I still remembered the law of probability from that last Maths period of school and knew we would be able to talk soon.

Thanks to being ignored and left alone to take care of myself. Literally.

And we did talk. Maybe a hundred times, till he started emotionally blackmailing me to let him come to my house at night, after everyone slept.

As you know by now, I had this knack of inviting trouble and you would think I had learnt my lesson by now, but this was one game I just had to play. We plotted and planned the entire meeting, accounting for my family's schedule, including the time Abbu returned from work, had dinner, watched TV, took a walk around the compound, then coffee before finally dozing off. Plus, provision of an extra hour for contingencies. After making sure that the coast was clear, I would signal Deepak from the window and leave the front door open for him to sneak inside . . . If only I could have applied my mind like this in school as well!

That night Abbu returned home late. So the whole schedule went haywire. Dinner got late too but Abbu's ever-increasing blood pressure made him a bit too disciplined about the walk. After coffee, Abbu decided to take out his bad day at work on little Rashid, who got beaten up to encourage sleep, but I think it charged up Abbu even more. Because I thought I could hear some strange noises from Abbu and Ammi's bedroom for a long time.

It was probably 2 am when I could signal with the torch to poor Deepak standing patiently down below, near our building, for more than two hours. My heart was almost pounding out of my best nightie – baby pink with small purple flowers. Slowly he opened the door and let himself in. Even in the dark, I could feel his intense gaze moving all over my body. He held my sweaty hand and I started shivering with excitement but was I fully prepared for what was going to happen next?

Bang. Lights on. *Sau sunhaar ki, ek louhaar ki.* Abbu's one slap across my face was enough to make me forget the hundreds of thrashings I had got from Ammi. Yes, that's when I understood that Allah made men physically stronger – even the weaklings. Game over.

MARCH 1996:

KARACHI, PAKISTAN

I went back to my country to attend yet another wedding. Mine. The Deepak episode had opened my Ammi's eyes. She knew it was time to take drastic steps or there was no way to prevent this *manhoos*, this luckless, wretched creature, from bringing utter disgrace to her family. So the very next morning she called up Khala and the rest of the clan to ask them to start looking for a boy. I was all of seventeen, like a ripe, tempting mango, and had to be given away to the rightful owner before I got too rotten to be devoured. She made it clear that the boy should be settled in Pakistan as she had decided to wash her hands of me, once and for all.

I was taken to a photo studio and made to pose in a traditional *sharara* and jewellery. The pictures were sent to all our relatives and in no time proposals started pouring in. With my kind of credentials, it was not so difficult. Fair, voluptuous, big eyes, only daughter, father working in Saudi, probably decent dowry. Own house in Karachi. The works.

This was my one big chance in life to some happiness. I blew it.

In my desperation to get married and get out of Ammi's house, I agreed to the first boy who demanded an early marriage and no dowry. I thought it was my way of giving back to Ammi who had brought me up with such hardship, but honestly have only my sexual urges and my age to blame.

I had not been allowed to even look at the pictures of the prospective grooms. Even then, the thought of having a husband would turn me on. I shamelessly insisted on getting married at the earliest. I longed for some male company, as both Omar and Rashid gave me no absolutely no love and respect. Ammi had ridiculed me and called me a whore so many times and so openly that I was almost treated as one in that house. I believed her too when she regarded me as a useless burden. She cursed the day she took me from Khala, thinking that I was God's gift to her. But all I turned out to be was a bitch in heat. They had stopped beating me but their abuses were enough to destroy whatever sense of self-worth I had. I really don't know what exactly I was looking for and how vulnerable girls are, thinking that marriage will change their destinies.

Wasim. This boy I chose based on his urgency in getting married. He was nearly thirty and after a broken engagement and a broken heart, fell in love with my picture. Adil Chacha's son . . . Sometimes I wonder if Ammi agreed only because of this reason. Even though she had not given birth to me, she really was my mother, after all.

Like Khala's family, Adil Chacha had left the discomforts of Lakkar Mandi and moved to Karachi a few years back in search of a better future. He worked hard and now owned a small grocery shop and a small house. His wife had done well and left him the proud father of four sons before she died. Still with a strong built and with a generous smile on a rugged face, he welcomed all of us, particularly Ammi, with open arms. I knew then that it was not just my imagination. He was the same Adil Chacha who filled the void Abbu had left in Ammi's life when he went off to Saudi. That Ammi and he had a history. But I wasn't interested any more. All I could think about was his eldest son.

Sawera's *shohar* Wasim. These three words were enough to melt my heart. He did not have to do anything to impress me as I already had surrendered myself to his being.

Now we all have watched enough Punjabi weddings in films so nothing that I am going to mention here will make any difference. Except that mine wasn't as lavish, obviously. So here I come straight to the point.

Suhaag raat. Sitting straight in that difficult position of having my feet tucked beneath those humongous hips, exactly in the centre of my shimmering green-and-silver *lehenga* that formed a neat circle around me, I looked with anticipation around this room which was supposed to shield me from my humiliating loveless life in Saudi. I was in my own country with my own people. Nothing could go wrong now. The cracked photo frame on those chipped walls, the broken chair and the shrieking bed didn't matter.

So he entered. The room first and then me. Just like that. No holding hands, no kisses, not even first removing my jewellery bit by bit, like they show in the films. Bang on target and left me with nothing but some blood to clean up after. And lots of tears. Mostly because it was almost impossible to get rid of those red stains on a white bed sheet.

That moment I just knew that I was truly *manhoos*.

Hazaaron khwahishen aisi ke har khwahish pe dam nikle
Bohat niklay mere armaan, lekin phir bhi kam nikle

The next morning, I woke up to the sound of Wasim leaving the room, banging the door behind him. I was too nervous to move, when I heard someone knocking softly on the door. Before I could react my venerable father-in-law came in. And got me a cup of Kashmiri tea, also known as *noon chai* – a pink traditional beverage with an exotic taste. The highlight of the day.

'*Salaam*, Sawera, hope you had a good night. You know your *chachi* left me alone to take care of these four sons of mine. I have tried my best but I am not sure if I could ever replace what a mother could have done.'

I had no idea where it was all leading but he then told me about what a pure soul he was, never thinking of remarrying, bringing up his children single-handedly while struggling to make ends meet. Of his days of struggle and what a self-made man he was, from being a street hawker selling vegetables to having his own small business. He then spoke about Wasim and how much his mother's death had affected him. Wasim was a loner and had no relationship with his brothers. With not much age difference between the four, limited means and no woman in the house to provide that soft touch, the brothers had grown up amidst bitter rivalry. They fought over everything. From toy cars to real bicycles, from a glass of milk to an extra piece of *gosht*, from tooth brushes to razor blades.

'Now you are the only woman who can bring some sanity into this house . . . Some peace and love. I trust you, Sawera, that you will be a loving companion to Wasim, a support to my other sons and a dutiful *bahu* to me.'

So with a brigade of five men in the house, I started wondering if I really was all that *manhoos*.

I decided to concentrate on my role as a dutiful *bahu*. My day would begin with the usual sound of the banged door. After a quick trip to the toilet, I would prepare tea for everyone. *Nashta* would be scrambled eggs, parathas and even keema on special days. Though Ammi had never allowed me inside the kitchen, Adil Chacha took it upon himself to teach me everything from scratch. He taught me to cook the simpler dishes like the *dal* and *sabzi* that Wasim preferred, as well as the complicated and savoury *nihaari* and mutton *korma* for the rest of them.

Though the boys were used to doing their own work, they now expected me to do everything from cooking to cleaning to laundry. They avoided talking to me but once in a while I used to catch them looking at my body. Specially the youngest man of the house. And the oldest too. Slowly I was developing a unique relationship with each.

Wasim. My *shohar*. Except for brutally entering me, sometimes even two or three times at night, there was no intimacy at all. Right after *nashta*, he went to work and returned late in the evening. I was not allowed to ask him anything: about his job, what he wanted to eat, about his broken engagement. The only three words he used to say to me were: 'You want it?' and before I could reply, I could feel his hands going down to my *salwar* and taking it off in a hurry. Such a puny, thin man, mostly on a vegetarian diet – I wonder where he got his stamina from.

Adil Chacha. My *sasur ji* had slowly started expecting a bit more than just three meals from me. I could sense his hands rubbing against mine for an extra moment while working with me in the kitchen. Mostly when we prepared the dough. How can this slimy mixture of flour and water be a turn on? No wonder these cookery shows on TV are such hits. I could sense his lips growing dry and heart skipping a beat whenever our hands would touch. If I wasn't having such a bad time in bed, I would perhaps have led him on.

Akram and Jamal. To them their *bhabhi* was nothing more than an attractive *kaam wali masi*. They were uncouth loafers who did nothing but spent all their time loitering with other young men in the *mohalla*. Adil Chacha tried all sorts of tactics from pleading to insults to get them to help in his shop but they had better things to do like playing cricket in the daytime and cards in the evenings.

Iqbal. The youngest of the lot. Almost my age at nineteen, he was the only sensible male in the family. He had just started college and was waiting for the day he would graduate and get out of his pitiful surroundings. And take me along. Or so I hoped. Because, it seemed to me, he wasn't man enough to try anything more than just looking at me. I was still a fool who had learnt nothing.

Well, I could be wrong. As all my life I have been used and exploited by my men so much that I have to sometimes remind myself that all are not same. So probably Iqbal was not interested in me. Difficult to accept but maybe that is the fact. But he was my only link to a civilized world. The only person in the family with some *tahzeeb* and who did not push me around. He was getting a little more open to me, too. Sometimes he would even get books for me to read.

Over time, Adil Chacha got a bit too possessive about me and gave me those dirty looks if he caught me talking to Iqbal. He even forbade me to go out of the house. I was like this local celebrity, a beautiful girl from a rich family in Saudi. Unmarried girls around my age tried befriending me but Chacha would be offensive to anyone who visited our house. I wasn't even allowed to go to Khala's house and he made his hatred for my family very clear to me more than once. He taunted me not bringing dowry. So what if they were not too direct about their demands? We should have understood. He called everyone names, including my Ammi and Abbu, who had not lived up to his expectations and had just washed their hands of me. Maybe he was right. As I hardly got any calls from Saudi.

Even inside the house, I had to always cover my head. I started feeling claustrophobic and dreaded washing those shirts, pants, *lungis* and undergarments belonging to Chacha and his four sons. I wished Allah had not listened to me when I longed for some male company, as just the sight of these five men together used me make me feel like vomiting. Especially if they were eating *aalu gosht*.

But when I missed my periods twice in a row, I knew why I always woke up with such a nauseated, sinking feeling in my stomach. Allah, please let it be a girl, as I cannot take any more males.

I had never felt so alone before. I called up Khala and asked her to go to the hospital with me. The lady doctor gave us the usual lecture about having a good diet of milk and fruits, lots of rest and daily vitamins. Khala was really worried: who would take care of me in that all-male territory? She called up Ammi to discuss my pregnancy and the plan of action. I have never understood Ammi, as she volunteered to come all the way to Karachi to look after me and supervise the delivery. I think she wasn't ready to give up her rights on me as yet. She was still insecure about Khala getting too close to me.

Chacha was relieved, as the prospect of a pregnant young girl in the house was making him nervous. His sons couldn't care less – maybe it wasn't such a bad thing, not having any other woman interfering. In our society it is not really a manly thing to get into the female domain of pregnancies or deliveries. Except for impregnating, they want to be kept out of everything. Still, a mother in law, especially in this situation would have made matters worse if she had to deal with my difficult mother. I went over to Abbu-Ammi's house in Karachi for the rest of my pregnancy, till the baby was born.

One. And two. Then three. Masha'Allah, in a span of two years I had three children. Had twin girls, the first time round. And then a little brother for them. Sana, Suhana and Naveed.

Ammi proved herself. I am not going to get into petty issues like not being given enough gifts on my deliveries as the fact that she was with me throughout each pregnancy was enough for me. Everyone appreciated her selfless act of so sincerely looking after her daughter who wasn't entirely her own. I know it would be a much more interesting story if I said that she ill-treated me or was hardly around for me or my babies, but when *qayamat* comes we are all answerable to the Ultimate.

It wasn't easy for my Abbu to arrange the money for her trips, but they did not let me down. Thankfully they had been able to built a house in Karachi few years back when they still had the money. As after I got married, Abbu's job had started to suffer. He was getting older and unable to work like before. His *arbab*'s business too wasn't looking good due to the never-ending rivalries between him and his brother. Then Abbu lost his job. And the company car. Still not wanting to leave the country, he accepted the first job that came along, even when it meant shifting to a one BHK and now having to walk to work in the heat. Maybe that was when they realized that I really was their lucky charm. But I was gone. Tough times for them. Tougher for me.

The relationship between Wasim and me went through some new lows. After Adil Chacha's heart attack, for which Wasim conveniently blamed my daughters, he was forced to look after the shop, as it was time to take responsibility of his own family. Anyway, his salesman's job hardly paid much, so he had no choice but to sit in the shop he hated the sight of, selling eggs and bread instead of credit cards. He would come home late, sometimes drunk, and take out his frustrations over having to haggle with illiterate women over the price of a packet of *chai patti*, on me.

So after working like a donkey looking after the house, my ailing *sasur* and three hyperactive toddlers, I had to present myself to my husband who was always very particular about his routine of first shouting at me, then beating me up whether I responded or not, then a bout of crying while apologizing and ultimately pushing me down to shake out the simmering liquid from between his legs. Of course, whether I responded or not. Because corpses don't.

I know countless books have been written about abused women and I don't want to belittle the circumstances of other women by comparing my plight with anyone, but to me this still wasn't the sad part. The sad part was yet to come. Again and again.

One more thing. I was abused but did not mind giving back when it got a bit too much. After all I had the protection of my youngest brother-in-law, who had the guts to shield me whenever my husband tried beating me in front of everyone. Now a graduate, he used to talk to me about sophisticated topics like politics, women's rights and corruption. I knew the day was not far when he would leave his *unparh* family for a brighter future. Unfortunately he did not find me, now a mother of three, appealing enough to take me along. I was too naïve to even wish for something so silly but it did come as a big shock for me when he suddenly disappeared. He had found a job in Lahore and one day left his helpless *bhabhi* to fend for herself.

The same night, when my husband pushed me on the bed, I took out a knife from under the pillow and dared him to come near. I was on my own and no matter what the cost, would not let anyone else dictate my fate any more. Though my children were too little to understand, these constant rows had started to have an impact on them, too. For their sake, it was time I learnt to survive. And for that I had to get away. Once and for all.

Because even Khala left me. The one who gave birth to me. My one chance of escape from this mental house, she died. Just like that. We don't know what really happened but one morning she did not wake up. Gone. No hints. No warnings. No goodbyes.

How was I supposed to feel? For the one who had abandoned me. For the one who never got a chance to show her love for me. For the one who perhaps never did love me.

But I was wrong. When I went over to her house for mourning, Khalu handed over a letter that she had left for me, the gist being that all her life she felt guilty for giving me up but at that time and under those circumstances, this was the best she could do. She kept herself away from me as she had taken an oath to never get emotionally attached to me as I belonged to her unfortunate childless sister. And she apologized and wished me well. I think that was enough for me.

But there was more. She had saved enough to leave a gold jewellery set for me, which Khalu said I was not supposed to show off and was for use only in case of dire emergency. Yes, they knew the day would come soon.

I started telephoning Abbu and Ammi more frequently in the hope of their asking me to join them in Saudi. When it did not happen for a long time, I started begging them to call me. I did not belong in this country. I certainly did not belong with this family. Abbu kept making excuses of not having enough money for the tickets or the paperwork being too complicated and lengthy as I was now married and had a different name. I needed a new passport too, as the old one had recently expired. Though he had a family visa, he wasn't allowed to sponsor his children once they crossed the age of eighteen.

I was desperate to get my life back and was ready to do anything to get out. And then he came in. Parkash Uncle, Adil Chacha's Hindu friend, a learned old man who could predict the future just by looking at some charts of the movements of the planetary systems. Usually he got mixed reactions wherever he went. Some genuinely revered him, some openly called him a fraud and some were too scared to challenge him. As soon as he entered our house, I could instantly feel a strong flow of energy. There was an aura about him which was very confusing as it wasn't all that positive. He was to stay with us for two days but then he saw me and his plan changed. He asked me about my date of birth and drew some geometrical figures on the paper, along with some strange calligraphy which was probably Sanskrit text. He told me to not worry, as I would be out from this house soon. When I asked him how and when, he refused to answer and reprimanded me for not believing him.

He then warned Adil Chacha and Wasim to stop ill-treating me or else this beautiful woman would run away and never come back. He specifically told Wasim to be gentle with me in bed and to take care of my sexual needs. He was right, as for me, there was nothing as repulsive as sex. Just think about it – a girl who, as a child, couldn't wait to be alone to be able to watch a blue film, who had the guts to call her boyfriend to her house one night, who got expelled from her school for writing love letters, turning out a woman who felt disgusted at the sight of her husband's naked body.

Wasim, in a weak moment, confessed that he was still in love with his ex-fiancée and did not feel anything for me except some contempt and lots of lust. But he turned a deaf ear to all predictions and joined the group of people who thought Parkash Uncle was a fraud. How wrong he was.

This 'fraud' had to prove himself. He told me that he would make sure I escaped from this house. Secretly he took me to the passport office as well as the embassy and got all paperwork done in order for Abbu to be able to arrange my travel to Saudi legitimately on a visitor's visa. The timeframe for such a visa is three months but I couldn't care less. Whatever it took, I had to leave from here.

Why was I so stupid to think that my life would get better in Saudi? What was I running away from? And for what?

When my new passport was ready I started calling up Abbu again to help me out, it was impossible for me to live in Pakistan. I missed Ammi just too much. And I was tired of getting beaten up almost every day. But each time, Abbu gave me no assurances. Only excuses.

After one such call, I was lying in bed with a severe headache, and after some wailing and beating my chest, was cursing the day I was born and pleading with Allah to finish my life, when Wasim entered. Drunk as usual but with bloodshot lustful eyes. He took off his *salwar* and stood in front of me but this time nothing happened. I laughed wildly, looking at the peanut between his legs, calling him a eunuch. I teased him even more by taking off my *salwar* suit and stood naked close to him. I started singing some sensual Hindi film songs and slowly moved my nails on his chest. When I came closer to kiss him, he called me a *randi,* pushed me hard on the floor and I hit my head on the bed. Feeling the blood, this time on my forehead, I still couldn't stop laughing, evoking a helpless fury in him. He stormed out of the room. Without raising his hand at me even once.

So if this was the best night of my married life, my resolve to get out became even stronger. No way was I going to live or bring up my children in this hell. Allah, help me, Allah. Where are you my *farishta*, the Arab in white clothes, I need you so much. Help me.

I woke up the next morning with Adil Chacha banging loudly on my door. He had just received a call from Saudi. Ammi had got paralyzed. Abbu was calling me, his daughter, to look after Ammi. They needed me. They loved me. They missed me. *Alhamdulillah.* You listened to me, Allah, but yet again you took it too seriously.

Since that night, Wasim started sleeping in the corridor. He started coming back later and even more drunk than before. About two or three times he brought toys for the children and on the rare occasions that he played with them, his voice would grow softer. Sometimes they all laughed together. But those few moments were not sufficient for me to start accepting him as my own. To me he was a socially sanctioned rapist and now he couldn't even be that.

Within two weeks, my visa was stamped, tickets were sent and I took my three little children with me. To *bahir.* Where I belonged.

My only regret being I did not probe Parkash Uncle to tell me how my life would be in Saudi. Thank God.

Adil Chacha and Wasim went to drop me to the airport. They were furious about the situation but equally frustrated, as they knew no matter how hard they tried, there was no stopping me. There was an awkward silence in the car and I could see Wasim wiping off his tears every now and then. My loathing was turning into pity for this helpless man who was losing his family. As the airport drew closer, he made no attempts to hide his tears and actually started howling, with his nervous children in his arms. The children got scared and started crying as they were not used to so much affection from anyone, including their bitter mother. And certainly not from this man who was hardly around. What is the use now, Wasim, as you have no one but yourself to blame? Adil Chacha then started reciting some verses from the Quran about mercy and forgiveness but I was not sure what the fuss was about. I was supposed to come back once my visitor's visa expired but in our hearts all of us knew what the chances were of that happening.

MARCH 2002:

King Fahd International Airport, Dammam, Saudi Arabia

I was back, and this time I could not take the immensity of this airport for granted. On my last flight to Pakistan, I had never really noticed the numerous noisy cafeterias, hi-fi restaurants, sparkling duty-free shops, shiny toilets, internet cafés, money-exchange booths and even banks. But now I could not take my eyes off this grand airport, which some say is almost as big as the neighbouring country of Bahrain. Certainly much bigger than Lakkar Mandi, where I was born.

This was the time when mobile phones had entered the market but could not be afforded by people like us. Either the super-rich owned them or professionals who got them from their companies. Parkash Uncle had one but I never saw him use it. I also know that some affluent people in Karachi showed them off through the windows of their swanky cars. But they were still not as lucky as me, who was now in a country literally oozing wealth and luxury. This was the first time I saw a woman's purse costing more than what Wasim probably made in a year. Even the Arab salesman of that posh purse shop was talking on a mobile. If only I hadn't been so immature as to say yes to the first proposal that had come my way, and had waited some more, who knows I might have been approached by one of these millionaires in the airport. Maybe I still had a chance. On my walk to the customs, with three little children in tow, I started imagining a young, kind-hearted Arab falling in love with me and then accepting me despite my baggage. And gifting me that Louis Vuitton on the wedding night. Yes, I had still not grown up, even after mothering three children. Yes, hope was all I had. And my beauty.

I jumped with joy when I saw Abbu waiting for me right outside the terminal gate, with an empty trolley in his hands, in which he placed my suitcases along with my three children. He did not look all that excited to see us all. Perhaps Ammi's sickness had really pulled him down. I told him not to worry as their daughter had come back. I guess I was the only one really happy at the moment. Maybe Abbu was just too exhausted and in no mood to welcome his grandchildren. Though I knew it was coming, I did not want to face what lay ahead and I diverted my mind towards those tall buildings made of glass, and thought of nothing else.

Al Khobar is just about a half-hour drive from the airport. All this time, I could not stop thanking God for bringing me back home to these familiar roads. But Abbu nudged the taxi driver to go in a different direction from where I had last lived, to a shabby locality with some old buildings and random independent houses enclosed within walls as high as ten feet. Almost a scene out of that *mohalla* in Karachi. I did not have the courage to enquire about it and just let him lead the way. When we entered this tacky olive-green building with the paint peeling from most places, which did not even have a corridor or a lift, I knew I had jumped out of the frying pan straight into the fire. OK, I will make it easier for you – *asmaan se gira, khajoor main atka*.

I thanked my stars a bit too soon for not having to climb up a flight of stairs along with my loaded suitcases and sleepy children. When we entered the flat on the ground floor, it was so dark inside that I could not see properly. When my eyes adjusted to the new surroundings, I realized that this flat had been converted into a hostel of sorts. Every room had wooden partitions, creating smaller rooms, one of which was for two bachelors who shared this accommodation. I knew that Abbu had lost his job and moved to a smaller place but I could not imagine in the wildest of dreams that it was this bad. Before I could ask anything, Abbu took me straight to Ammi's room and I saw this sickly old woman lying on the bed, with unkempt grey hair, lips hanging slack from one side of her face, crushed under the weight of a blanket and her miseries. She was holding rosary beads, loosely hanging from her left hand – the side that still worked. Being a new mother, I was used to the smell of urine but on an adult, it is unbearable, just like the public toilets in Pakistan. Yes, now this was to be my new job and I had better accept it soon.

The room where I was to live with my three little children had a single bed, no cupboard, a study table which was to become the place to dump my suitcases, no chair and no privacy. There was only one bathroom for the four of us. And I am not even counting my three children here: Omar still lived with his parents. When I protested, Abbu gave me a look that basically meant that I had asked for it. Even if he had called me to look after Ammi, he was still doing me a favour. As things were not the same as before.

Little Rashid, now grown-up, had left for Pakistan to pursue higher studies; I was sure that in no time he would be begging Abbu to call him back. Omar had found a job in a nearby computer shop with a really impressive designation – hardware engineer. But by now I knew that all that matters is the money you earn, as Wasim, too, who, as a credit card sales executive in a bank, had earned not even half of what he did, sitting in his father's small grocery shop. As expected, Omar, who made hardly any money, wasn't too happy to see me in the house, as he couldn't care less if Ammi was taken care of or not. He gave a cold reception to his small nieces and nephew who were too innocent to understand the family dynamics.

I had practically no time to reflect on my situation as I got busy from the very moment I entered Abbu's house. My days and nights were devoted to giving medicines to Ammi that included some pills for anxiety and insomnia as well, giving her a bath, brushing her teeth, her hair, changing diapers, cleaning after her, changing her clothes, reading her blood pressure and giving her whatever emotional support I could. Not much of the last, as honestly I too was fighting my lone battles. Slowly I forgot all about myself and Ammi became the centre of my attention; I was the only one she could count on and I did not want to let her down. Perhaps I could win her love once again. So all my energies were directed towards making Ammi get better and every day I started noticing subtle improvements. I became obsessed with her condition. My poor babies were left to fend for themselves and apart from giving them food, I left them to take care of each other. Perhaps a part of me knew that the sooner they became independent the better it was for them.

A month passed and then two. No way, Allah, this could not be happening. I don't want to sound ungrateful to Allah about this but when I missed my periods the second time in a row, I was sure: Wasim had planted his seed in me just before he lost his manhood. Allah, I was not prepared and I was sorry but I did not want this! And definitely not now.

My visa too was going to expire but I begged Abbu to get me an extension. Ammi had improved but no way could she be left alone. She still needed me. I begged her to fight my case. I could not go back to that man who had never shown any love for me all this while. I told her about how I used to get beaten up and forced upon in bed every night. I dramatized my version of the story and converted Adil Chacha and all his other sons too into depraved, horrendous wild animals who could not control themselves if they ever saw a female. I wasn't safe there, Ammi, please don't send me back.

She didn't. She gave an ultimatum to Abbu that whatever the cost, Sawera should not be sent back. I don't know if it was out of pity or love or if she just needed my company.

So I could stay for another three months legitimately in this country. My pregnancy was showing and Ammi could now walk around and go to the bathroom alone. So I did something that was going to change my fate forever.

I went *bahir*. On the road, all on my own, and walked straight to the school from which I was thrown out some years back, thanks to that love-letter scandal. I went to Principal Madam's office and as luck would have had it, she invited me inside when she saw this sad familiar face with dark circles under her eyes. I told her that I was the same Sawera Aslam Sheikh who was expelled from school for writing a letter to a boy. I begged her forgiveness and went on about how sad my life had been since that incident. I attributed everything that went wrong in my life to that punishment, for which I was still paying (of course, very conveniently not telling her about some more adventures, like calling my other boyfriend home, leading to my parents marrying me off at such an early age). The poor vulnerable woman felt sorry for me and asked me what I really wanted from her. I begged her for a job, any job – a teacher, a receptionist or an *aaya* who changed nappies in the nursery section. It didn't matter. I did not want to be a burden on Abbu any more, and with three children and a fourth on the way, I needed a job very badly.

If only, if only I had not written that letter. If only I had continued my studies. If only I had not married Wasim. If only I did not have so many children. But it was too late.

Principal Madam sent me off, saying that she did not have a suitable position for me. But she took my number and assured me she would call up if anything came up. You know, basically, what that means. Allah, what could I do, no education, no skills, could not even speak English properly. What could I do? I slept, mocking at my future. That night my *farishta* came in my dreams, dressed in white as usual.

Next morning, the call came. It was Principal Madam herself, who asked me to see her in the afternoon. Allah had listened to me; I would have a job soon. I started planning my meeting with her and rehearsing about the class I would be comfortable teaching and how much I loved children and how thankful I was to my school. When I told Abbu, he gave me that sarcastic smile again and asked me to forget about it as who would be mad enough to employ a *jahil* like me.

If only I could prove him wrong that day. Whatever I imagined it was going to be, I could never have been prepared for what was to happen next. She handed over a sealed envelope to me, saying me that it was a contribution from the teachers and students of this great school. I was asked to open it after reaching home. I couldn't wait to get home and now that I had some money, took a taxi back. When I opened it with trembling hands, I thought I was still dreaming. I counted the deck of notes again and again and again. It was 12,000 riyals. About a couple of *lacs* in Pakistani currency. How could this be possible? As they say, *Allah meherban to gadha pehelwan.*

When I came back home, I was shaking violently with exhilaration. I showed the money to Abbu and Ammi, who choked up with tears. We kept thanking Allah the Merciful for listening to this sinner, this wrongdoer, this unfortunate Sawera.

Now I had enough money to pay for the visas for myself and my children and for the birth of my fourth one.

I have heard that some women go into depression and have mood swings during their pregnancies. I could not afford such luxuries. I was too busy looking after Ammi and my three children to even think about how I was feeling. I don't remember ever having an emotional outburst or even a bout of crying during those months.

Will you believe me if I said that Wasim, the father of my children, did not call even once, even when Abbu had informed him of my pregnancy. While I did not really miss him, I did think of him a few times but I was too much in denial to worry about the complexities of our married life or if we had future together.

The windfall brought a new energy to the house. Abbu had started to bring toys for my children, he took them to a nearby park to play and Ammi started fussing over me. Now she could work in the kitchen and would sometimes prepare soup for me. Even Rashid used to enquire about my health when he called. We were a family, after all.

However, my happiness was short-lived. Omar Bhai got a marriage proposal from Pakistan. That too Khala's youngest daughter, Alia – my real sister! How could they give two of their daughters to the same family? Was Khalu so blind to my plight? Didn't he realize by now that Abbu was not the rich relative from Saudi, that he was as ordinary and as middle class as all of them back in Pakistan? I had to do something to stop this marriage. I could not afford to have another version of me go through the same fate. Why could they not find a nice, responsible boy from a decent family in their own country itself? And why was I jealous to see Ammi so excited at the prospect of having Alia come to their house?

I called up Khalu and after exchanging those usual pleasantries, warned him against getting Alia married to Omar who was an unfeeling, cold-hearted man, who did not exactly have a good income, either. I told him about the condition of the house, with its partitions, a matchbox for a kitchen, a single bathroom for all, and bachelors I bumped into all the time. Well, not entirely true as I hardly got to see those bachelors from Africa, even when I was really curious about them. Khalu, instead of taking me seriously, accused me of coming in the way of the happiness of my sister, who deserved to get out of the country, just like me!

I tried to reason with Ammi too; I thought she would listen to me, now that we were closer. But, like Khalu, she too charged me with being a stumbling block in the way of any good things happening in the family.

My sister was coming into this house but still I was feeling alone as hell. In a way, I was feeling threatened about my status – after all, I was just a 'made-in-China' daughter who could not compete with the real wife of their 'original' son. Even if it happened to be my own sister, Alia.

As those wretched days turned into weeks, and weeks into months, I had to gear up to face my fourth delivery. Alone. Literally.

The date of marriage was fixed and it very conveniently clashed with the date of my scheduled Caesarean. The baby was head-up with feet hanging down, I mean, it was what the doctor called a 'breech baby' and a heavy one too, causing distress to his already stressed-out mother. More than physically, I was too low emotionally to argue with the him and gave in to his recommendations. Moreover, nobody was ready to take any responsibility, nor was anyone qualified enough to challenge the doctor's orders.

Ammi, who was absolutely fit now, turned a deaf ear to my appeals. Though it was to be my surgery, her heart had become anaesthetized towards my situation. Who would take me to the hospital, who would look after my babies back home? How could they be so insensitive? They brought me up, even if I was not their blood. How could they leave me back in Saudi to attend Omar's marriage? Why couldn't it wait? Were my children, my health so trivial, was I so second-rate, so worthless?

Ya Allah, who am I . . . where do I belong, where should I go?

Two weeks before the scheduled operation, when the tears streaming from my eyes could still not drown my sorrows and helplessness, I felt a gush of warm liquid down my legs. The bag of waters had burst and soon those all-too-familiar piercing pains followed. That fateful day, my family was still with me. I was rushed to the government health centre with Abbu and Ammi at my side and Omar volunteering to stay back home to look after my children. Thank God for little miracles. They were not really bad people. Perhaps as confused about my identity as I was.

Within hours, of which I have no recollection except those blinding lights above my head in the operation theatre, my youngest one, Aftab, came in this world. I was not a first-time mother, but each time is different and it gets more difficult with each child. Maybe at twenty-four I wasn't that young any more.

But Ammi looked after me. For a good four days. As soon as I got discharged from the hospital, it was made only too obvious to me that the holiday was over and I had to get going with my usual duties. Barely able to get up from the bed, with the excoriating pains of my stitches and a worn-out spirit, I had to hold on to life. I wanted to die but the thought of these four lives kept me alive. I started missing my home in Pakistan, my Adil Chacha and his Kashmiri *chai*, his love for food, Wasim and his comforting beatings and how much he cried when I left the country. And here I was – unwanted, unwelcome and redundant.

I announced that it was time to go home. I would accompany them on their way to Pakistan, attend Omar's wedding and get my life back. I was certain that Wasim would surely forgive me and slowly everything would get back to normal. I didn't care that my baby was still too small to travel, I knew my children were strong and could withstand any hardships, just like their mother.

Strong and gullible! When I called up Adil Chacha's home to speak to Wasim, he informed me that there was no use coming back now. Unless I could accept Wasim's new wife. The same girl who had broken her engagement with Wasim, to elope with another man, richer and much older. This old man had now died and the girl came back crying into Wasim's arms. Adil Chacha was totally against this alliance but he had to save his suicidal son, who was undergoing treatment for the depression he was suffering from, thanks to his first wife.

Now I had the answers. I was nothing. I didn't belong anywhere. And I had nowhere to go.

So Abbu, Ammi and Omar left me. How alone I was. With four children. And two bachelors in the adjoining room.

I was able to recover somewhat from the bruises the operation gave me, but the news of Wasim's new marriage had shattered me from inside. Yes, I didn't love the man but he was still my husband.

Now I badly needed another man. To help me. To comfort me. To earn for me. To give baths to my baby. To change the baby's nappies. To go to the store and bring milk for the children. To feed them. But more than a man, I badly needed to sleep.

To make things worse, I developed an infection in my stitches and had to take antibiotics and painkillers. As Ammi's self-appointed nurse, I had learnt a few things myself. But these medications used to make me drowsy and I wondered if fatigue and depression were its side effects.

A tired, weak mother, dirty starving children and no food in the house – I could not do anything but pray. It was then that I religiously started – five times a day. In good times and bad. I finished *Asr*, my afternoon prayers. The children were whimpering with hunger. There was no way I could walk all the way to the local store for milk or food – I could barely stand.

Though it was strictly forbidden for me to talk to or even look at these men who lived in the adjoining room, separated by a flimsy wooden partition, I had to turn to someone for help. I gathered whatever little strength I had and went straight into their room. I wished I had knocked but I wasn't really in my senses. I was just a mother. So I thought I could get away with anything.

Big mistake. Two men stood facing each other, ready for combat with their erect weapons, sizing up each other; tall as palm trees, shiny coal-black skin, and stark naked. So those men who had no other identities except as bachelors who shared the rent of this accommodation, were not all that single after all.

I fainted. Of shock or weakness, I still cannot tell. When I opened my eyes, I found myself in a nearby nursing home with one of them sitting next to me. I was being given glucose and there were some fruits on the bedside table, along with some medications. Before I could open my mouth, I felt a knot in my stomach – where were my children? The dark man told me that the children were safe at home with the other man in charge. The children were fed and sleeping. He told me not to worry as his partner was a qualified nurse and knew how to take care of a new-born. I had severe anaemia along with dehydration and had to be treated in the hospital for a day or two. And that was just the physical symptoms. Women like me, who had no support system, did not have the luxury of having emotional issues like extreme loneliness. I knew that for the sake of my children, I had to take help from wherever it came. I poured out my heart to this man from Africa, our gay flatmate who just sat there listening with open ears and closed eyes while the other one stayed at home to look after my children. I had no choice but to trust these two well-built black men to take control of the situation. One in the hospital and the other one at home.

I stayed overnight in the hospital, resigning myself to my situation. I could not call Pakistan, as they would blame only me for my miseries. Actually I was not so miserable any more as this one night had been a break that I so desperately needed. At last I had some other people making decisions for me. Whose names, even, I did not know. I didn't care as since then I just called them brothers. Did it make any difference to my feelings towards these kind men because they were not like the rest of us? Gay or not, I will be grateful to them for my entire life but I dreaded thinking what would happen if anyone knew of their sexual preferences, where we were.

The next month was not that bad. I was running out of money but every now and then, the bell would ring and I would find some bags full of grocery items like bread, eggs, milk, Farex, chicken, oil, soap, diapers, sanitary napkins – everything that I needed. Sometimes even more. Somehow the word had spread in the compound about this young woman with four very small children and no husband, and parents in Pakistan. Sometimes, the ladies would come from the neighbourhood and talk to me. Some tried finding out more. I did not let anyone down. I would share my story with anyone who cared to listen and I did not know where to stop. I did not mind the attention I had started getting, even if it came sometimes from sympathy and mostly out of curiosity. Yes, beautiful women always have that advantage. Especially beautiful young women having no male protectors.

Sometimes the bell would ring and random men from the area would try enquiring about my health and if I needed something. Usually they brought a couple of milk bottles or chocolates from the cold store which I gladly took. I never let any man enter the house, though, as I had other things to worry about.

My visa that was about to expire. Abbu and Ammi were coming back from Pakistan soon. And I had no money for survival.

With my three children in tow and the newborn in my arms I walked out of the house. I had a plan in mind that, against all odds, I thought would work. I walked down the streets to a nearby beauty salon. While I got my eyebrows plucked I observed the place. A giant poster of the Indian diva Madhuri Dixit adorned one wall and a row of mirrors another. There were a million beauty and hygiene products on display. Lipsticks, eyeliners, mascaras, blushers, nail polishes, concealers, massage oils, lotions, shampoos – you name it. Along with a milky-white Lebanese receptionist, there were about five or six attendants who were performing various services like waxing, threading, facials, manicures, pedicures. The customers were mostly Saudi women, mostly middle-aged; a couple of them very stylish with hair cut in short blunts and wearing smart, colourful dresses. It was an unbelievable sight, as till now I had seen them only in black *abayas* and *hijabs*. I couldn't help noticing their waxed, shiny legs on stilettos that had animal prints or fur on them. Some brought their small children along with maids in uniform – mostly Filipinas or Indians. The attendants were all Indians, too. They are everywhere.

Thank God for it, else I would have major language issues. While I was brought up in Saudi and studied some Arabic in school, I did not know the language too well, as usually people from one nationality do not socialize with another. But North Indians make great friends with Pakistanis because of the common culture and language. Malayalis are a different variety altogether. They are the most educated of the lot, so look down upon Pakistanis and Bangladeshis and if at all have to make associations outside their clan; would prefer the westerners. A mix of Hindi, Malayali and Arabic is the official language of Gulf, especially amongst expatriates. Everyone has these words in their vocabulary, like *Salam Valikum* (*As-salamu 'alaykum* or Peace be upon you – the usual greeting), *bhaiya* ('brother' for the random male worker), *yala*, let's go (come on let's go), *mafi mushkil* (no problem), *habibi* (loved one), *shukran* (thank you), *khoboos* (bread), *khali-walli* (let it be), cold store (small grocery shop). The commonest being *Insha'Allah* (God willing). So practically everyone can get by with just these ten-odd words.

I started a conversation with the girl who was very neatly plucking each out-of-place hair from my eyebrows. With a thread clenched between her teeth she couldn't answer me except with an occasional 'Hmm . . .' Except when I asked her if it was possible for her to help me get a job in the salon. She enquired if I had any certifications. That is the thing with Indians. An average Indian has half a dozen of them. They plan their qualifications, their careers, their marriages, their children and their lives. Unlike us.

What could I say, it was more embarrassing to disclose the fact that I was a school dropout than to ask her for *any* job – even a cleaner's. I told her I would do everything, from dusting, to cleaning the bathrooms to sweeping the hair off the floor to washing their dirty towels with traces of wax or dead skin on them. I could even attend telephone calls. Yeah – that I was experienced in.

The owner was scheduled to come anytime for her regular afternoon visit, so I was asked to wait. But with four restless children, I had to go back home and promised to return in the next few days.

My family came back. My adopted brother had got married to my real sister and I was not part of the ceremonies. I had been such a fool to think that they would postpone the wedding by a couple of months because I wasn't in a fit state to travel. If they could leave me with a week-old baby, then I was the stupid person here to think that they could postpone the wedding by a month or two. When they came back, they got some clothes and sweets for my children, which some relatives had sent for me. Ammi said everyone enquired about me and missed me and my children dearly. How could I complain when everyone meant so well? And hating them could only make things worse for me, so I took the initiative of calling everyone in Pakistan to thank them for their gifts. I also spoke to my younger sister to congratulate her and said something about all of us eagerly waiting for her to come to Saudi, once her papers were ready. I especially thanked Fatima, my elder sister, for fulfilling my *marhoom* Khala's duties in her absence, so well. You see, Fatima had got married to a well-settled man who worked as a government clerk. I had a gut feeling that it was time to make peace with everyone.

Life mellows you down and makes you humble. Even when you know the other people are just out there to get you, you still have to accept them, as in your heart you know that everyone could prove their usefulness one day. I don't know if it was humility or manipulation but I had to change myself to survive. I had to get on my feet, and soon. Otherwise my children and I would always be at the mercy of this family which had disappointed me time and again.

But for the time being, I needed them. I told Ammi that an old friend from school had got me a job in a salon and I had to join soon. I would leave the toddlers at home and was allowed to keep my baby with me. When she asked me what I would do, I lied that it was a beautician's job. They would first train me for a month and then gradually let me deal with the customers independently. I made up all kinds of stories about the salary and the tips I could make. I assured her that there would be no trouble as my barely five-year-old twin daughters were mature enough to take care of themselves and their brother. Ammi gave in on one condition – that I would quit the job if she could not manage the children. Maybe she thought the extra money would bring some respite as Omar's wedding had left them with enormous loans on their heads. As I said before, we do not plan.

Next day, with my baby in a flimsy old pram donated by the lady next door whose baby had outgrown it, I went over to the salon where my so-called school friend had arranged that prestigious job for me. Though covered in black from head to toe, with only my eyes showing, I felt a sense of freedom I never knew before. I found myself humming old Hindi film tunes as I walked to the salon, some twenty minutes away from our compound. However, I entered the salon amidst commotion. I saw the beauticians clustered round their colleague in the centre, a short dark girl who was howling that she did not do it. A Saudi customer had accused the girl of stealing her diamond ring, which she had taken off while getting a manicure. The receptionist was frantically asking the customer to calm down and wait for their Madam. In five minutes their Madam stormed in – a tall woman with a tough face, probably in her fifties. I couldn't help noticing her navy-blue silk blouse, crisp black trousers and red lipstick. When she spoke, everyone listened. She asked the customer if she had really looked hard. The customer started babbling about the exact place she had placed the ring, just next to the hairbrush on the dressing table. Madam politely asked the customer to check her bag again. The customer claimed to have done it and kept talking about dragging that poor girl to the police station. Madam smoothly took the bag from her hands and sure enough, the ring was found in the bag. There was an awkward silence before the customer apologized, collected her belongings and walked off from the crime scene. On her way out, she pushed a of ten-riyal bill into the girl's hands. The price of a poor person's self-respect.

Madam comforted the crying girl and told everyone to get back to business. By now, I was too intimidated by this lady with red lipstick to be able to open my mouth. I looked for the girl who had plucked my eyebrows and asked her to recommend me to her Madam. She hardly knew me but she did. She introduced me as her friend and requested Madam to give me a job. I narrated my plight of having four children to feed, and even how, though I came from a so-called good family, I was forced to look for work.

She hired me. Just like that. No questions asked. Without any certificates. With my baby. As a cleaner. My first job: 10 am to 7 pm, Saturdays to Thursdays. Salary of 500 riyals or about fifteen thousand Pakistani rupees, a month. By Saudi standards it was too low, but I could now pay for the visa extension and still have money to get diapers and formula milk. And an occasional taxi to the salon if it got too unbearable in the heat. *Alhamdulillah.*

Once, while walking to the salon, I could sense a car following me. I could hear the faint honking but I kept walking fast. I felt the car stopping and the taxi driver came out running to speak to me. He told me that I had dropped my purse on the road and he was just trying to help. I thanked him for my empty purse. He tried making some small talk but I just hurried off. I was too scared of being attracted to his kind old face with gloomy drooping eyes. And to his taxi – a brand-new white Toyota Camry with a glistening orange roof.

Of course, it had to happen. When we met again on the same route, he asked me if I needed to be dropped. Like those rich salon customers,

I ordered him to pack up the pram and keep it in the car boot while I sat behind with the baby. The first three times I paid the taxi fare.

So, every day exactly at 9:45 am, I had a taxi waiting for me a little distance from the compound gate as I did not want anyone to find out. Hamid. The Saudi taxi driver. A tall man usually dressed in a grey *thobe*. I did not tell him the exact nature of my job and he did not seem to care. For him I was just a pious young woman who needed some support. And he was more than willing.

He didn't like to talk a lot but told me a few things about himself. Even at forty-five he had remained unmarried after the death of his young wife who left the world while delivering their first child. He had lost both. And all hope to any happiness. But a self-made man, he drowned himself in his profession, driving his taxi, sometimes in two continuous shifts. Hard work had paid off and now he owned his own small transport company with three taxis and one mini bus in its fleet. He told me what a lonely life he had with no friends and no one to look after him; especially after the recent death of his old mother, he was completely alone. He used to thank God for having found me. Maybe he was moving too fast as I was not sure if I was ready for another relationship. Especially when I was still married to Wasim.

For the first few days, he was just a taxi-*wala bhaiya* for me, a bit more considerate than most. Even after struggling so much in his life, he was not bitter and was open to new things. New things, such as making a mother of four fall for him. And he did a good job of it. Every morning he would bring a red rose for me and greeted me with childlike excitement. He always took the longest route possible to the salon and sometimes I would get a few minutes late. With romantic films songs playing in a plush air-conditioned car, he did not have to try too hard. We didn't talk much but I think those were probably the best days of my life so far, as I got not only love but respect from this man who had never tried taking advantage of me. As yet.

One day he asked me to meet him on Friday morning, promising a long ride to King Fahd Causeway – the picturesque bridge on the serene blue waters of the Arabian Sea, connecting Saudi to its friendly neighbour, Bahrain. To get out on a Friday, which is a weekend and an off day across the Gulf, was an impossible task but as I said before, love always finds a way. Now, I am not one of those rich sophisticated women who discuss the true meaning of love in salons. For me it was love enough if a man was ready to take responsibility of me and my children. Though he had not yet promised anything, I knew that it was bound to happen. Rather, I had to make it happen.

So Thursday night, just after the *Maghrib* prayers, I went to Ammi and told her a lie about my Madam asking all the beauticians to do an extra shift as she was organizing a complete treatment of facial, wax, massage, makeup and all, for the ladies in her coffee-morning group. There was no way that I or anyone could refuse. It would be just a few hours and I was specifically asked not to bring the baby along. I exaggerated about how rich Madam's friends were, their chauffeur-driven cars, about their embroidered *abayas*, exotic *ittar* (scent), blonde hair and the kind of tips one could make. Ammi, impressed with my narrative of a job that included being in the company of the super-rich class, encouraged me to go. I made a mental note in my mind to give her some cash when I came back home, saying it was the tip I made that day. That would silence her from asking any questions. Because I myself had a lot of questions in mind.

As I dressed and got ready next morning, I wondered what I was doing there. What do I expect from this man? Does he really care for me? What does he really want from me? And what will happen today? I went out to our usual spot round the corner, from where he used to give me a ride to work.

Hamid was standing by the car, holding a bouquet of red roses. I had a sense that it was going to be the ride of my life. Hamid, dressed in a crisp white *thobe*, was a sight to marvel at. A brownish stubble on that fair skin, those gloomy eyes that had a new twinkle this morning, broad shoulders, a mobile phone in his hands, black leather sandals; what more could I ask for?

Like a newly married couple, alone for the first time, we both felt an electrifying current in our bodies when his hands touched mine to hand over the flowers. Too awkward to say anything, Hamid started fidgeting with the music system to play the usual romantic Hindi film songs.

It took us about half an hour to reach the toll booth at the start of the bridge. We were asked to show our *ikamas* (Saudi registration or identity card) or passports to the official. Wait, Hamid's passport looked almost like mine – same deep-green cover and Islamic Republic of Pakistan inscribed in gold. Hamid was a Pakistani? This man, who talked like a Saudi, walked like a Saudi, looked like a Saudi, was a Pakistani like me? My dream of getting a permanent Saudi residency was evaporating in the thick air of the Arabian Sea!

After the formalities, we were soon on that grand stretch of wide roads, overlooking crystal-clear waters merging into the blue sky above. When I asked Hamid about his passport, he told me confidently that he considered himself a citizen of Saudi Arabia. His parents were from Pakistan but he had never been to that country and was actually in the process of acquiring a Saudi passport. It was just a matter of time.

Now time was something I did not have. I had been living in this country on a visitor's visa for almost a year and I knew I could not get lucky each time. I was perhaps the only person in the history of the Saudi visa control department, who got extensions three times in a row. Every time, the old man in that office would take pity on me and let me stay on for another three months. By now, I had become an expert in narrating the sad story of my life, to my advantage. It usually worked but I could not count on my storytelling skills and a stranger's vulnerability to keep going indefinitely.

I had planned on getting married to this Saudi taxi driver, getting naturalized and then living happily ever after in this land. I had nowhere to go to in Pakistan, my so-called homeland. Khala was no more and the rest of my brothers or sisters could not care less. I could reconcile with Wasim and live as his legitimate first wife. But I would not go back to the place from where I had run away. My children and I deserved better.

With all these thoughts racing in my mind, I was taken aback when Hamid asked me to marry him. Just like that. Without even the customary 'I love you'. He assured me that he would honour me and accept me fully along with my four *masoom* children. He would make sure I never had to work again and would love and bring up my children like his own. Oh God, I wanted this so badly but how could I take the risk with someone whose papers were still 'in process'?

Of course, I said yes. To wait for a real Saudi to fall in love with me enough to want to get married was a chance I could not take. Yes, I was impulsive but I had neither the time to think it through nor a lot of people to take advice from.

So, on our way back from that romantic drive, Hamid took me to celebrate to a place he called his home. It was an old building with service apartments that you could rent for a month or even a day, if you knew the manager well. By now, I had seen enough of life to know what this was leading to. We went up in the lift to a room on the seventh floor. A maroon carpet, dim yellow lights and a bed with heart-shaped pillows; this was going to be my day, after all.

I went to the attached toilet to freshen up, apply some more lip-gloss and some more perfume to camouflage my nervously perspiring underarms. I took off my *abaya* and *hijab* before coming out in my pink sleeveless *salwar* suit with a low neckline, revealing the deep cleavage parting my spongy flesh. I found him sitting on the blue velvet sofa. He asked me to sit next to him. He held my hand and kissed it softly. The next moment his lips were on mine and I gently guided his shaking hand from my shoulders down to my bosom. He tried removing my *kurta* but it was so tight that I had to shamelessly volunteer for the task. He took off his clothes, (over) confidently tried lifted my not-so-light body with a jerk, clenching his teeth, and arranged me neatly on the bed, simultaneously unknotting the string on my *salwar*. Everything was happening in slow motion except that by now I was getting impatient. Perhaps I was too used to Wasim's hurried lovemaking, so that instead of savouring these moments, I could not wait for it to get over. Maybe the extra guilt was adding to my impatience or maybe, like me, Hamid also could have done with some more perfume on his outrageously hairy body.

After an hour we were back in his taxi and he dropped me home. Imagine what he must have felt when I asked him for some money. I didn't feel the need to explain that it was supposed to be the tips I had got in the salon for my overtime, which Ammi was probably looking forward to.

Since then it became the usual thing every Friday. Our coordination got better and I started looking forward to these long sessions of making out, rejoicing in the heavy petting, and pleasantly surprised by how much I had started to enjoy it. It was not as good as what I saw in porn videos but it was close. Except that my man did not wax his body. Like they say, beggars can't be choosers, so I did not have high expectations, anyway.

Ammi stopped bothering as the 200 riyals at the end of the day shut her up. I knew that in order to ensure my stay, I had to move fast.

By now I was the proud owner of a mobile phone. It was a surprise from Hamid, in the middle of our lovemaking, perhaps to titillate me even more. When I looked at this shiny pink marvel between my breasts, there was no stopping me and I ended up making him a very happy man indeed.

It was time to use the damn thing.

I called up Wasim and demanded a divorce. He refused. He called me names and said that he would never let go of me. He screamed into the phone that he wanted the children back and would cut me into a thousand pieces if he ever saw me. I knew by now that he was a wimp and that a few threatening phone calls would suffice to fix him.

Wasim said the word *talaaq* three times on the phone the day I got my fourth and last visa extension. I was a divorced woman, with four dependents and an indifferent family. Both times I cried but I cried more when I realized that I did not have a husband any more. And I cried even more when I thought of how fine I was cutting it.

All I had was three months.

Three months of customary mourning or the *iddat* period after *talaaq*, in which women are supposed to live modestly, stay covered up and not mingle with other men. They are not usually allowed to work unless they are the only source of income for their families. I had no choice but to continue working.

Three months till my last day of stay in Saudi; within which I had to make arrangements to get a permanent visa. But before that I had to make sure that my divorce papers came through and I acquired the status of a legally divorced woman. Though typically, it's the man who has the right to the children, in this case Wasim wasn't man enough to even put up a fight. He washed his hands of us and thought he would finally have a peaceful family life with his new wife and yet-to-be born children. Big mistake.

However, I couldn't care less, as my own plan was to marry Hamid as soon as he got his Saudi passport, become a legitimate citizen myself, get my children adopted by him and live happily ever after. The most over-used phrase.

Two months passed. His papers were still in process. Whenever I asked him, he would shrug it off, saying that he was trying his best with whatever contacts or resources he had. He could not really get it that it was a critical situation for me. I did not want to pressurize him any more for fear of pissing him off. I needed him. As my husband. As the father of my children.

One Friday, when he parked his car near the compound gate as usual to drop me off, I asked him to come inside. No more hiding. Ammi and Abbu had to know. I politely told him that it was time he asked their permission to marry me. His face turned red and he started mumbling about not being prepared and did not want to go empty-handed. That was when I knew that he was perhaps an even a bigger wimp than Wasim. I went off towards my building without even saying goodbye. But not before taking the usual tip.

I came home and got busy with cooking, cleaning, feeding my children, telling them stories of little fairies who lived in palaces made of chocolates and who spent all their time playing, chasing butterflies and dancing in magnificent gardens full of red roses. And then I thought of the red roses Hamid used to bring for me, I looked at my thin children with their pale faces, old clothes and broken toys. Whatever it took, I could not let them down.

Next Friday, I did not get out of the house. I could see from the window his car parked for almost an hour before leaving. In the evening he called me many times on the cell phone and each time I would disconnect the call. When Ammi enquired about why I did not go for the overtime, I told her I needed a break, too. She did not take it too well and started complaining about the rising cost of mutton. Well, sorry, Ammi, I don't have those 200 riyals today.

The next morning, I decided to walk to the salon. I did not give Hamid a second glance when he came out of his car to talk to me. He kept asking me why I was being so difficult and that he was still working on his papers stuck in the Pakistani Embassy and some more rambling about true love. I told him very firmly, imitating my Madam's style and body language, that I would talk to him only if he came home to ask for my hand in marriage.

For a whole week, he kept calling me but I did not answer. I had to prove to myself that I was not a toy, especially not to an old Pakistani taxi driver. Also I had started getting nervous about the whole situation. With my days numbered in Saudi, I could not depend on Hamid to show his manhood. And I certainly could not depend on him getting Saudi nationality soon. For all I knew, it could be a long and tedious procedure and usually these requests are rejected. I had to do something. And soon.

I discussed this situation with my Madam at the salon. I narrated my whole story to her and my pledge of not going back to Pakistan as I could not afford to feed my children there. There were no jobs for an uneducated woman like me and no place to stay, either. I had my brothers and sisters but the relationships were too complicated. Obviously I could not take the risk of a second marriage, as the chances of a divorced woman with four children finding a remotely decent man were close to nil.

She listened carefully and seemed touched. Despite being a staunch businesswoman she had a reputation of being very kind-hearted. I had heard that she also ran an NGO for women who were victims of physical abuse. She donated benevolently to orphanages. Surely she would take pity on me.

Eight thousand riyals. She demanded 8000 riyals in cash. I could not believe my ears when she told me that she would sell me a work visa for two years. *But Madam, I work as a cleaner, I hardly make any money, I have four children to support. How can I arrange this kind of a hefty sum?* She was in no mood to negotiate. She would apply for my work visa. I still had to go back to Pakistan as I could no longer keep my dependents in this country. She would send me the visa there. No commitment on paper. Just good faith.

She also told me that perhaps it would be a good idea if I married a Saudi man in due course if I had to keep my children with me. Yes, I had a Saudi man. Almost.

I badly needed advice this time but who could I turn to? I spoke to the beauticians in the salon, who were apprehensive about interfering in my affairs and offending their Madam. I contacted the neighbour who had donated the pram to me. She told me that Saudis, depending on their businesses, are allowed to grant work visas, but sometimes their employees do not work directly for them. They buy the visa and are then free to work in more lucrative jobs, with their sponsor's consent. The sponsors make a neat profit on them, charging sometimes double or triple of the actual costs they incur as processing fee to the government. These visas are typically known as 'Free Visas', meaning freedom to work outside. Not totally legal but accepted, nevertheless. As long as the employee did not act smart or indulge in criminal activities.

Oh yes, I remembered the part-time maid we had a long time back, she too said something to us about her being on a *free* visa.

With just a week to go, I could do nothing but agree to Madam's demand. I knew that it was time to let go of the only inheritance I had – the gold set Khala had left me – surely it was worth even more .

After selling the set and handing over the money to Madam, my new sponsor, I still had about 2000 riyals to meet my expenses in Pakistan for the next few days. Till I came back.

Meanwhile, Hamid kept calling. I kept my word by not talking to him. I was bleeding from inside as I knew this relationship was on the verge of ending but I still had a spark of hope. The *iddat* was almost over and I had a flight to catch on Saturday. Should I meet him for the last time this Friday? I prayed and prayed for a solution as I still did not want to let go of a man I had such hopes on. At the same time, I was not a whore. Yet again, I had to prove it to myself.

Friday morning, just after returning from our prayers and settling down to have lunch, we heard a knock on the door. I ran to open it as I immediately knew Allah had once again answered my prayers. Hamid came but not alone. He got a *qazi* with him.

He introduced himself to my startled Abbu and Ammi and right away asked for my hand in marriage. I thought I was going to get beaten up again but this time, perhaps they were too shocked to react. The discussions went on till the evening, with Abbu embarrassing me no end. Everything rotten about our lives was spilled out to Hamid. Including my adoption, their lack of money, my failed marriage, my nomadic temperament, and the four innocent little victims of these circumstances. Hamid listened and listened. And then he got up from the sofa. Like a leader delivering a speech, with folded hands, he started by greeting everyone once again. Then he announced that he was not interested in my past and now he would give me and my children the future we deserved. He promised them that as soon as his papers got through, he would send for my children. Same old living happily ever after. Just the way I had imagined, though with some minor complications. He consolidated his act by putting a gold ring on my finger and seeking the blessings of the elders – my parents, Abbu and Ammi.

Clapping would rob this moment from its seriousness so all we did was hug each other. Everyone in the room cried, including the *qazi*. Here was the greatest deed ever being performed – an honourable man taking a destitute woman under his wing ... *Nikah* ... *Qabool hai* ... show over.

As I said, Allah always takes me too seriously.

The next morning, I left Saudi. Overwhelmed with this new feeling called security, on being married with the man who loved me enough to give me 2500 riyals for my expenses, I was flying in the air. Literally. But even more heavenly was blowing up a few bills in the duty-free shops. I bought the famous Ajwa dates, a silver pendant with Rumi calligraphy, a *kaftan*, some key-chains and dry-fruit-filled chocolates. Thank you, Allah, for my husband. My Hamid.

MAY 2003:

KARACHI, PAKISTAN

I knew the news of my marriage to a rich man had reached them all, when I saw a familiar face waiting anxiously near the Arrivals gate. Fatima, an older and plumper version of me, was standing there along with her own catch – the famous government clerk for a husband. He took the trolley from my hands and started leading us to the taxi stand, making his way through the crowd. Millions of men, women and children, cars, autos, cycles, buses – so this is my country. I realized that I was actually soaking in the sights and the scents, just like those rich foreigners.

We reached Fatima's home where Khalu was waiting for all of us. Along with my other brothers and my younger sister Alia, Omar's wife. Looking genuinely happy, they welcomed us all with open arms. When I looked at Khalu's wrinkled grey face with bushy eyebrows, orange teeth owing to those countless betel leaves, and greasy lips, I looked upwards to say a word of thanks that I had taken after his wife and not him, otherwise I would have had no chance to make it big. As if I had.

My love-starved children bonded with my family in Pakistan as if everything had always been good. Naturally, they were oblivious to the history, the internal tensions and the backroom politics.

Everyone gathered around me when I opened my hand luggage. I took out everything unhurriedly, one by one, and each time there was a collective sound of cheering. But when I declared the box of honey-coated cashews as the last gift, I could sense some disappointment in the air. Yes, the insatiable hunger for mobile phones back home!

Fatima's husband Shahid Bhai seemed like a no-nonsense, serious sort and kept away from us all. I liked the way he appeared indifferent towards his prettier sister-in-law and the gifts she had brought. Fatima told me that marrying into his family was not really a good move as he was one of the honest, incorruptible types, so it was rather difficult for them to make the ends meet on his meagre income.

Some more gossiping and some more idle talk. Away from Ammi and Abbu, in my own country with my own people, I was actually getting that feeling of belonging, which had always eluded me so far.

Hamid. Oh, in my excitement to meet my family, I had almost forgotten about him. I called him to tell I had reached and he started whispering back about how much he missed me and he could not wait for me to get back in his bed. Men.

Fatima and I had a lot in common: same eyes, same lips – but she had lost her small waist to two children. Her husband was one of the few men in our community who did not act on impulse and was content with having two girls. Her home was a small comfortable shell and they seemed like a content family. Except Fatima, who was like me. Too ambitious. And too restless.

The next morning, when I handed over some money to her, I saw her face light up at the sight of shining crisp Saudi notes. I asked her to get them converted into the local currency and keep them for my expenses while I was there. She hugged me while blessing me with abundance in wealth and happiness. By now I knew that this is how a person buys love.

In order to sustain this love, I had to play along to also sustain the impression they had in their minds about me. That I was married to a rich taxi driver with his own business, who would soon get Saudi nationality. That he would keep sending money all the time my children and I lived with them. Having worked in the salon, I could now pretend to be a stylish woman who knew about makeup trends and some expensive brands of perfumes. Fatima was my most eager student and loved listening about the high-class Saudi life, their expensive cars, six-lane highways, gold and oil. We bonded over tales of Saudi's affluence.

A month passed. Then two. I was now left with very little money to survive and under no circumstances could I let them get a hint of my reality. I called up Hamid and asked him to send some money, which he promised. I called up my sponsor to enquire about my visa, which she promised.

Another two weeks passed. Hamid did not transfer the money and nor did my visa come. I knew my sister was too greedy to tolerate me even for a day without being paid. Perhaps I was to be blamed for spoiling her but it wasn't really my fault if I was brought up without some family values. I had to keep Fatima happy if my plan was to work.

Which was to go back to Saudi on a work visa, be with Hamid, get Saudi nationality automatically as soon as Hamid's papers were through and then send for my children. My children would stay with their loving Khala Fatima till their own papers were ready. Of course, for a price. One might think that I was being a very unfeeling mother but I had to keep Hamid motivated too, as I did not want another case of *out of sight, out of mind*. I could not let him forget about my sensuality, or the adorable little children that he had promised to adopt and take full responsibility for. I had begun to feel jittery. But all I could do was pray.

Allah, *Al-Muhaymin,* has never let me down. Just when I was on the verge of giving up, the money came. And my visa too. It was time to celebrate. We arranged a mini bus and went on a two-day expedition to Gorakh Hills and rejoiced among those tranquil lofty peaks, those breathtaking sights and chilly winds. I had to bring the family together and make them pledge their devotion towards me. A beautiful setting almost guarantees it. Yes, I invested all this money as I had to buy Fatima's loyalty before I could ask her to keep my children with her while I went back to Saudi. It was a risk worth taking. Honestly, I did not have another choice.

As expected, she refused. Which idiot would take such a responsibility? Four extra children to look after, to educate, to provide for, four extra mouths to feed! Her husband would never ever give his permission. What was I thinking?

Sixteen thousand rupees. Four each. I put the deck of notes on the table and asked her to think hard. I promised that I would send this amount every month as expenses for my children. She told me it was not enough. We settled for twenty thousand. Five each. Final. Now it was not my problem if her husband agreed or not, if he beat her that night or threatened to divorce her. A deal is a deal. Just like Ammi and Khala. I knew when Fatima gave her word she meant it. And I meant it too when I promised to send the money regularly. Basically we both were our mother's daughters.

Little did I know that I would not be able to keep my part, as when I went back to Saudi, all hell broke loose.

AUGUST 2003:

AL KHOBAR, SAUDI ARABIA

This is one trip of my life that I don't remember anything about except that I did not stop crying even for a minute. My poor babies were at the mercy of their cold-blooded *khala*, someone who was just in for the love of money. I thought of the naked fear in their forlorn faces, when I bid goodbye to them at the airport; the loud wailings of the older ones and those confused eyes of my baby haunt me even now. My heart was breaking with an acute feeling of helplessness and resentment. Which mother would be so brutal? Why, God? How did I end up here? History was repeating itself. I had still not learnt my lesson and was doing exactly what my mother had done to me. But here, it was going to be different. I took a holy oath in my mind with Allah as my witness that I would bring them back. Whatever it took.

An oath that I was not able to fulfil. As I said, all hell broke loose.

In Saudi, it is customary for the sponsors to go receive their employees at the airport and do the necessary paperwork, otherwise the employees are not let out. For a long time, my eyes were searching for Madam but obviously it wasn't easy to make out which one was mine. So when this tall woman, dressed in black with only her eyes showing, approached me, I looked up to say a word of thanks.

I was supposed to go with her to the salon, call up Hamid who would get me from there. I forgot to mention that Ammi and Abbu had told me very categorically that they would not be held responsible if anything went wrong in my life when I decided to marry Hamid. It was purely my personal risk. The usual attitude with love marriages in orthodox families. For the sake of courtesy, I still had to inform them about my arrival. They again reminded me that now it was only Hamid who was my *sarparast*, who had the right to steer my fate in whatever direction he wanted. If only he was man enough to do it.

One whole day in the salon and there was no contact from Hamid. His cell was unreachable and I had started panicking. What if he had met with an accident? What if he had lost all his interest in me? When it was closing time I pleaded with Madam to let me spend the night in the salon. My husband was in trouble and my parents had cut off all ties with me. I had nowhere to go. It was just a matter of this one night.

We both knew that it was not going to be this one night. When there was no trace of Hamid for the next two days, I changed into my cleaner's uniform and got going. I had to feed my children back in Pakistan and had to be strong as always. I knew by now that it was stupid to depend on anyone else to fulfil my children's dreams. And I wasn't even thinking about the castles made of chocolates. Now it was all about food and shelter. Surely I could provide them with these basics.

I also persuaded Madam to let me learn the tricks of the trade and if she felt I was trained enough, she would let me handle the customers independently. I started assisting the beauticians in odd jobs and observing their demeanour. I learnt that attitude is more important than skills. The most sought-after beauticians were the ones who were mostly smiling, who greeted their customers with genuine enthusiasm, who listened to their problems, who offered tips – from applying makeup to oiling hair to skin treatments to taking care of children! The customers came here to feel good about themselves and their lives, and now it was up to us to make it happen for them. The salon was a happy place, buzzing with a constant flow of energy and the incessant sound of hairdryers.

Two months passed. I was still living in the salon. Though I was under training, women had started preferring me to the other girls. Not because I was more skilled than them, but because Allah had given me the courage to rise up to the occasion. I pretended to be a happy-go-lucky woman who loved serving others. Maybe I did. The facials, massages, pedicures helped me take my mind off my sorrows. I did not have the time to worry about the complexities of my life and whether my children were being take care of or not. Whatever money I made, I used to send to Fatima, who had no clue that I worked like a donkey and had no husband any more. I still had no idea where Hamid was. Even if he was dead, I could not care less. He had deserted me. And I needed this to take complete charge once and for all. No more false hopes. Even when I did not have a concrete plan about the future, the onus was on me. Everything would be all right. Or so I thought.

Early one Friday morning, my cell phone rang and instinctively I knew it was Hamid. I ignored it. After several calls, I had to answer him out curiosity if not out of any concern. He kept saying sorry and begged me to meet him outside the salon. He told me that he was in big trouble and had not really abandoned me.

Hamid took me again to the same apartment building. He apologized profusely and gave his version of the story. He told me that the night before I landed in Saudi, he got into an argument with one of his customers in the taxi. This customer was a rich Indian businessman, who had contacts higher up. According to Hamid, this vicious Indian was probably just playing on his own anti-Pakistan sentiments as Hamid had done nothing to provoke him. He made a police complaint and got him arrested on the charges of physical assault. Hamid was in jail all this while before finally getting acquitted two days back. He was not allowed to make phone calls from the jail and thus could not reach me. I wanted to believe him. Women.

The next morning, I woke up in his arms. It had been the most unbelievable night of my life. I was with the person who had not forgotten me and still wanted me. He was to go to take permission from my Madam to let me live with him. Of course, that was the plan. By all means, I was his legitimately married wife. But there was one small hitch. I had to continue working in the salon. Those last two months that he spent in the jail had rendered him penniless and it would take a while before he got his reputation and old customers back. Like a virtuous wife, I understood him. And supported him too. Emotionally and financially. I did not even enquire about his fleet of taxies as I didn't want to put him off and neither did I really understand the intricacies of business.

Though I was earning just about enough through my salary and tips to support my children back home and take care of my personal expenses, it was not sufficient to take care of the added burden of Hamid. He could barely pay the rent but I did not call myself a virtuous wife for nothing.

Door-to-door servicing. By now I had made some contacts myself. These rich women who used to come to my salon would sometimes enquire if I could visit them in their homes for these beauty treatments. Some of them were too old to move, some did not have the time to come and then wait for their turn, some had driver issues and some were not really permitted to go out of the house. But they all still took good care of themselves.

I did my calculations and realized that I could make twice as much by serving just half as many customers on my own. I bought a professional vanity case and some salon supplies. Thanks to a taxi driver for a husband, I had no transport problem, either. I had a list of customers who wanted to be served at home and they all promised me that they would build up my business, in return for some free treatments. At the same time, it took me longer than it should have as I was worried about antagonizing my Madam. I knew she would not approve. If I started without taking her permission, she would probably get me thrown out of Saudi. But then I thought of how she sent me the visa, even when she had no legal obligation to do so, just on good faith. I would go and ask her. Yet again, I was counting on her magnanimity.

Five hundred riyals. Every month. If I was to be on my own, I had to pay her a monthly tax of five hundred riyals. It did not matter if I had customers or not. Else she would not allow me to work outside. *But Madam, I was told that having free visa means the right to work anywhere, even other than the sponsor.* Yes, that is usually the case. But not in this case. Who would compensate for the customers I would steal from her? Did I think my Madam was a fool? She knew everything, including my so-called secret intentions of starting my own services that I used to discuss with the regulars of the salon. Of course they were not all that loyal to me. Why would they be and lose this chance of some more idle gossiping with other ladies in the salon, including Madam. A free pedicure is not always enough to stop wagging tongues.

But I thanked God, nevertheless, for this lady who wasn't really being so unreasonable. Of course, she had her own business interests to protect.

With basic equipment in my bag and Hamid as my driver, I could now fix up my own appointments. If only it was that easy. One whole week passed. Then another. I was now jobless and spent my time calling up the same loyal customers to fix up with them. Yes, I said loyal as I got nothing. Their loyalty lay elsewhere. Hamid had also started taunting me about my overconfidence and seemed rather happy that my strategy was not working. That was also the beginning of the sourness in our relationship.

Then one day a call came. It sounded like an Indian voice, and she wanted to meet me. When this lady came to my house, she introduced herself as Geetha. Striking big eyes, coal-black hair and dark skin, resembling those voluptuous Malayali film heroines, except that she was too short. Or else she would have made it. Coming back to the point, she told me that she too had worked for my Madam about four years back till she decided to be on her own. Her story was almost like mine, only less complicated, with no divorces or children in the picture. She had to support her family in Kerala, including her brother, who was still in college, and an unmarried younger sister. She had come to Saudi on Madam's work visa but she realized in the ensuing years that she was going nowhere, with no chances of getting her salary increased, so she decided to break away. Madam let her go under the same condition of five hundred riyals a month. She underwent a lot of struggles finding customers but later realized it was Madam who had hinted to all the ladies who visited the salon to stay away from Geetha, who was rumoured to be a petty thief, having stolen some random items like lipsticks, accessories and hair brushes from the salon. It was Madam who spread stories about Geetha having flicked her customers' money and jewellery.

Now everything was making perfect sense to me. I used to wonder how Madam could let me break away from her so easily. Whether I succeeded or failed, she would still gain. She knew that it was not entirely impossible for me to find customers but she tried delaying it for me as much as possible while guaranteeing herself five hundred riyals as a monthly penalty for daring to rebel. Oh Madam, I underestimated you.

Geetha told me that for a year or two, she had been working independently. But in a few months she would be leaving Saudi for good, as conditions at her home had improved. By then her brother would have found a job and her sister been married off. Her fiancé had promised take responsibility for her ailing mother. Also, she was an educated Keralite and would prefer to start a business back home. So there was no point staying back, except that in this short span of time, she had made a fortune in Saudi, having some of the wealthiest women among her customers. Customers she wanted to keep even in her absence. She was looking for a reliable partner who could carry on the legacy and, in turn, split the profits when she was gone. Being called reliable was a beautiful feeling but how did she know? She didn't. She was just taking a chance as she mostly took all decisions instinctively. Just like me, the only difference being that she was never wrong. And I am not going to get into the story of how she got her hands on my number – it is not important, really.

What is important is that from now I was under some serious training. For the first few weeks, she took me everywhere with her. We would start in the morning and finish sometimes at midnight. The fact that she could speak English with an American accent made a big difference in the way people treated her. She told me to keep picking up and soaking in everything – her dainty mannerisms, her telephone etiquette, her designer clothes beneath the *abayas*, her branded shoes and bags, everything. It was the whole package that counted. Quality was everything, being genuinely interested usually worked and if the customer was still not satisfied, a neat discount did the trick. A beautician not only has to be a skilled professional but a fine actress, a psychologist and still be full of interesting stories, to be successful.

Yes, interesting indeed, as you may have thought that Saudi is the most conservative country in the world, where women have no rights and are treated as prisoners in their own home. But the women I dealt with were some of the most adventurous, daring and independent I had ever seen. And I had seen a lot: the women in my Ammi's circle and the women from the rich class. And I have lived almost my entire life in Middle East. So I know.

I am not into sensationalism and will not talk about alcohol, drugs, dating or wild parties. But thanks to my profession, I got to see a different side to Saudi than the world perceives.

I never ever got eve-teased, whether I walked to the market, the school or the salon – whatever time of the day or night, it might well be the safest place for women on the roads. Thanks to the law of the land, it has a negligible crime rate and rapists are almost always given capital punishment. If life was so difficult in Saudi, do you think expatriates would constitute a third of the population? And I am not talking about the poor labour class from the subcontinent. Saudi is also full of western expatriates who work as consultants, doctors, bankers and some very qualified Indians who leave only on retiring.

Then the sought-after private compounds. Yes, in the middle of Saudi Arabia are these fascinating oases of spacious freedom that seem unbelievable the first time. Mostly built for and rented out to expatriates, you will see women in shorts lazing by the pool or taking tennis coaching, driving their SUVs and dropping children to playschools within the compound.

Geetha had the privilege of access to many such compounds. The difference between life inside boundary walls and the world outside seemed too stark for the women there, especially the newcomers. But slowly they learnt to make peace with their circumstances and almost all the women I met enjoyed their time in Saudi.

Of course, the luxury of beauty treatments within the privacy of their homes helped. Geetha and I became close friends. She was a mature and more glamorous version of me and did everything it took to fend for her family. Except for her dark skin, I wanted to be like her in every way. Maybe I would have if she had stayed back for some more time.

I learnt so much from her but will never forget the most important lesson: that the ultimate goal of any beauty treatment is that the woman should feel more confident about herself. If makeup does not deliver, your compliments sure will. But don't overdo it or she could get suspicious. And that would be sad. So spread happiness. Make every woman believe that she is the most beautiful in the world. And stick to the rich; don't waste time over the middle-class aunties who never seem to be satisfied. And business will boom. It did. Naturally. Happiness meant having five hundred riyals at the end of the day.

About six months later, Geetha packed her bags and left the country for good. We had no contract between us and I was under no obligation to split my profits with her, but she was like my sister and not for one second did I think of betraying her trust. I fussed over her and bawled on the way to the airport but she seemed to be calm for such a situation. When it was time to say goodbye, she told me that she was leaving me behind to carry on the tradition. I promised her that I would share a part of my earnings with her as long as I was in Saudi. She smiled at me because she knew.

That one day Hamid will make it impossible for me.

I wasn't entirely surprised when Hamid started showing his true colours to me. The free food in the jail and his wife's earnings had gradually turned him into a lazy parasite who liked to blame me for his worthlessness. This driver had lost any drive he ever had or the need to be out in the streets looking for customers. His only job was to take me to customers' houses and wait shamelessly for hours till I finished my routine. I had learnt to ignore the pangs of worry or suspicions that were building up inside me. Did Hamid really own a transport business? Why didn't he come out of the jail any sooner if he had contacts? Didn't he have friends in this country? At the same time, I had completely drowned myself in my work. At least he could give me a ride whenever I needed and be available to satisfy my insatiable lust. He might have lost his passion for work, but his passion for me was enough to keep us both going. Sometimes he would massage my aching body after a long day and make me ache for more of his touch. He would also prepare tea for me and treat me to those famous *baklavas* from a nearby sweet shop, especially if I bought a pack of Marlboros for him. I was too busy to fully understand that each time he made tea for me his ego would get submerged in the hot cup bit by bit. Still, deep inside I knew it was only a matter of time when his machoism would haunt him for being dependent on a woman to survive. However, I was on a new high: when a customer passed on a shiny bill of Saudi currency to me, when I sent some to my children, when I bought beauty supplies, when I gifted a new cell phone to Hamid from my own money and when I sent Geetha her share.

My business was growing. I had managed to get some affluent women as my patrons. Women married to rich powerful men did everything except housework to sustain their relationships and were obsessed about staying attractive to their husbands. Most had an impressive staff of maids, drivers, cooks, nannies, tutors, etc. They lived in palatial bungalows with manicured lawns, swimming pools, tennis courts – straight out of that Indian filmmaker Karan Johar's movies. Some of them were very generous with tips, especially if they got complimented by their husbands. Some were not so kind, maybe frustrated about their rich, lonely, empty lives. Some were naturally beautiful, some not so lucky. But all had one thing in common. Insecurity. Of losing their men and territory to younger, more attractive women. And thus becoming an unwanted first wife.

My job was to stop it from happening. And so far, I was good at it. Till one day, I noticed my customer's husband eying me from a distance. Usually I never really got to cross paths with the man of the house but for this particular customer, it was becoming routine. When my customer, a seemingly lovely woman who rewarded me generously, eventually stopped calling me for my services, I knew that I was still paying a price for my looks. When it happened a couple of times more with other customers, I started wondering if I was the one putting out mixed signals to men. Yes, I realized that if I had to go far with these women, I had to stay far, far away from their men.

As I had my hands full with my own man back home. Hamid was showing signs of restlessness with me. He would be shamelessly sarcastic whenever I entered home with more money than usual. But there were some days when he was utterly romantic and decorated our bed with red roses to entice me. Then there were days when he vanished altogether. On being confronted he used to blabber about staying at a cousin's or a friend's. Or taking his clients on a visit to Bahrain on weekends in his taxi. I believed him as I desperately wanted to see him getting out of his shell and helping out with running the house and taking responsibility. It was not for my four children back home but because I had to provide for my household in Saudi as well. The rent, grocery bills, petrol, his cigarettes – all came from my earnings and despite earning reasonably well, I started wondering if getting married to this worthless swine was a good idea, after all. Especially when he refused to part with the money he made on his frequent so-called trips to Bahrain. I was confused about my relationship with this man who was giving me mixed signals.

The day he declared that his application for Saudi citizenship was rejected, I knew I was in a really big mess. I was blind not to have seen it coming, as despite hearing that it is literally impossible to attain citizenship of this country and happens only in the rarest of rare cases, I still believed that Allah would grant this wish to me. It was the only way I could bring my children here.

With time, I realized that I was being naïve thinking of reuniting with my children. I had to go back if I had to be with them. But I was married here. I had my own life, my own husband, my business. I decided to stay in Saudi and keep working even harder to save as much money as possible so that my children could have a good life in Pakistan. Till I figured out a way to get them here. If that was not being naïve, then what was?

This. One day Hamid confessed.

After a particularly wild session of uninhibited lovemaking, with his release he screamed out her name. Crying profusely, cursing his misfortune, beating his forehead, he had no choice but to tell me. That he had another wife. And three children. Right there in Saudi. All this while. When he followed me in his taxi on my way to the salon, when we went to the Causeway bridge, when he promised to look after me and my children, when we made love for the first time, when we got married in Ammi's house. When I blushed thinking of my new husband, when we fought, when I got cigarettes for him, when he made tea for me. He was married all along. So he went to his first wife and children on the pretext of taking his clients to Bahrain. Now I knew I was really naïve. And stupid. Cursed. Helpless and really, really *manhoos*.

He told me that he was indifferent towards this frigid old hag of a wife. Despite having no sex in the relationship, he could not leave her as she had no one but him. That his children deserved to have their father, after all. That he in fact was in love with me and wanted us all to stay together as one big happy family. What a vicious joke life was playing on me. By now I was numb with pain. I felt my heart was broken in a thousand pieces, I felt humiliated and used. And totally indifferent to this man, I stopped believing him too. Except that even though he called out her name during climax, I still wanted to believe that his first wife was actually a frigid old hag.

The fact that I was an independent working woman (yes, I love using this phrase), made it easier for me to demand a divorce. So after a week of locking myself in a darkened room, crying my heart out till I had no more tears left in me, I went up to him and asked him to set me free. I could no longer stay with him and had my own children to think of. I had my customers who were waiting for me. I had to grow my business. And that was the first time in my life I felt I did not need a man. Of course, life can be surprisingly brutal, as even after this incident, I continued to be used and abused by men. Actually, many of them.

Hamid refused to let go of me and kept pleading with me to forgive him. But my mind was made up. And I was not as helpless as he thought. I still had my family in Saudi. Abbu, Ammi and Omar would definitely rise to the occasion and support me in these trying times.

But they did not get that chance. Before I could even go to them with my miseries, Abbu died.

My poor Abbu just collapsed at the gate of the compound, on his return from his morning walk. Peacefully and without any fuss. And with his death, Ammi's fate was sealed. She no longer had the right to stay in this country and it was time to return to her motherland. Omar had his own employment visa and seemed relieved to be finally able to live a hassle-free life with his new wife, away from the constant quarrels of a joint family over money, space and household duties. Rashid was studying, staying in a hostel in Pakistan, and refused to be with their mother. Ammi was discarded by her two *jawan hatte-katte* sons. She would move to their house Abbu had built for retirement in Pakistan. Basically it meant that I, too, had no one to depend on now. When I went to drop her to the airport, I knew she was as helpless as me and too weak to take any decisions about our lives. When she bid a tearful goodbye to me, I felt terribly alone and extremely exposed.

At the same time, I was in two minds whether to live with Hamid and accept his other wife or to be on my own – a thought that seemed scary but exciting.

As usual, I – rather, life itself – opted for the 'exciting' choice of moving into a shared accommodation with one of my customers, an old Indian lady to whom I had got close. She lived with her husband in a company villa. The couple's grown-up sons were settled in America, so they were just passing their time in this country till the husband's retirement from the law firm to which he had given his golden years. When she heard my story she asked me to live with them as she needed company and welcomed the prospect of having me in the spare room of her house. Actually it was the 'housemaid's quarters', which were now mine as Aunty mostly did all the work herself. With a single bed, a TV, cupboard and an attached toilet, it would do for me. The rent was to be a weekly session of massage while lending an ear to the tales of her younger days and her properties in Kerala. The couple was rich, kind and took pity on this woman who slogged her way to provide for her four children in Pakistan. It did not matter to them that they were Hindus and I wasn't. In the Gulf, Indians and Pakistanis live together in peace because all they are interested in is making a living without any trouble. Some of them sustain their association for life, even after they go back to their respective countries.

Gradually I started to feel comfortable in my existence. My landlords insisted I called them Aunty and Uncle, which felt awkward at first but gradually I started basking in their warmth. They missed their children terribly but had resigned themselves to the fact that the lure of America would not let them come back. Every evening, I would find Aunty waiting for me on the lawn and she did not approve if I got late. Sometimes, we had lunch together, usually comprising their all-time favourites, fish curry with coconut gravy and *appams*. And they both talked non-stop. I had nothing to give in return, except listen to them over filter coffee.

However, Hamid started stalking me and threatened to make it very difficult for me if I did not go back to him. He was a spineless creature and I did not take him seriously. Big mistake. Because men don't have to do a lot to ruin a woman's honour. *Randi*. Yes, Hamid accused me of prostitution and threatened to tell everyone what I 'really' did to survive. If I did not let him back in my life, he would make sure that I would rot in jail for committing a heinous crime that is completely unforgivable in this country.

For a long time, probably more than a year, I tried ignoring him and carried on with my life as usual; I lost track of time with my customers. I was bleeding from inside but spread happiness wherever I went. My appointment diary was full of these ladies waiting to be pampered. One of them introduced me to Google, my best friend. Literally. Even though I was branded a *jahil*, an ignorant savage, all my life, I took to the internet like cold wax takes to unwanted hair. Because these ladies turned to me whenever they needed advice on acne, hair loss or weight. The irony being that they also sought me if they could not manage their little children or maids or mothers-in-law or even husbands. Imagine – me, who had made a mess of every stage of my life! Completely inexperienced but thoroughly knowledgeable, thanks to research, I was now an agony aunt on any topic under the sun. I became an expert on natural remedies and organic cures, too, for conditions like anxiety, depression, insomnia and even infertility. Sometimes I experimented on myself and soaked up whatever knowledge I could about women, life and love.

I was also building up contacts as I knew a day would come soon when I would need help in any form to attain reprieve from the biggest *faux pas* of my life – Hamid. Yes, I had a few French customers too!

Back home, my children were taken good care of by my elder sister, who bought a new computer, new curtains and new shoes for her own children. There is no dearth of gossipmongers in our society so I got regular updates from the neighbours I had befriended while I lived in Fatima's house. It did not really matter, as it was through Fatima's happiness that I could ensure my children's well-being. As long as money kept pouring in from *bahir*, it was fine with her and as long as they were fed and sent to school, it was fine with me, as in my heart I was praying for the day when I would be able to bring them to Saudi. Still, I longed to touch them, kiss their innocent faces and hug them tight, shielding them from all the brutalities and complications of this wretched world. The hollowness in my already aching heart used to get unbearable and often I would cry and whisper lullabies in my sleep, dreaming of a day when I would look after them, bathe them, brush their hair and cook *halwa-puri* for my precious little ones. Especially my favourite, my youngest baby, Aftab, who perhaps had already forgotten me.

By now I had learnt to take one step at a time. I was also living in fear: what if Hamid did spread false stories about me to this kind Indian couple? I had won their trust over time and just recently they had asked me to move out of the maid's room, into their guest room. I would be left with no roof over my head if these God-fearing, righteous people even got a hint of it. Till now they treated me with respect and admired my unbeatable spirit and commitment towards my children. But that was because they thought I was an honourable woman. But I was. Was.

One evening, when I saw them waiting at the gate, I knew Hamid had proved himself. They called me inside to have a talk but Uncle was very clear that I had to be completely honest. I told them I was just a beautician who did nothing but offer beauty services to ladies. I had four children staying with my elder sister whom I supported from what I earned in Saudi. Hamid was my second husband. I left him when I came to know that he already had a wife. And that he was a liar and a cheater. And that he was blackmailing me to go back to him. And I desperately wanted to break free from this malicious, spiteful, evil man. Exactly the story I had told them the first day. (*Yes, sometimes I had these strong sexual urges but surely that didn't qualify me as a prostitute, did it?*)

Lawyer Uncle listened for a long time and then gave his verdict. I was an honest, hardworking woman who had not committed any crime. If Hamid tried harassing me, Uncle had contacts higher up and would make sure this criminal would spend the rest of his life behind bars on charges of domestic violence and mental torture. I cried from relief. Allah not only sent these *farishtas* for me but I was now under their protection. I was no longer scared. And it was time to free myself from this claustrophobic marriage. Whatever it might take, I had to get my divorce soon.

Little did I realise that divorce was not going to be the only episode that would happen soon. In the next two days, my life was going to change. Forever.

DAY ONE

8 am: *Uncle's house, meeting my* **sautan.** After the first peaceful night in many days, it took me a while to register the sound of someone knocking at my door. Aunty informed me that I had visitors and that it was time to resolve my problems, once and for all. After a hurried trip to the bathroom, when I saw them, I knew that this was going to be a day I would never forget. The so-called old and frigid first wife of Hamid, with charcoal-black eyes smudged with kohl, deep-pink lips, a beautiful fair face and a well-endowed body in a figure-hugging *burqa*, introduced herself and her brother, the man sitting next to her. Uncle was taking stock of the situation and very politely asked them to continue, while I continued to stare at this beauty whose name Hamid had called out that night. Mehrunissa. I wondered what was more beautiful – her name or the woman herself. She looked shaken up, as she had just found out about his marriage to me. She started rambling about her being in love with Hamid and saving her marriage for the sake of their three innocent children and how they had somehow managed to find me. Because she could not talk sense, her brother, one of the rare cases of a Saudi citizen of Pakistani origin, intervened and asked me to leave Hamid. So this was where Hamid had got his inspiration for citizenship. But this sophisticated man was a government employee, law-abiding, highly educated, married to a Saudi woman from a decent, well-to-do family, unlike this crook his poor sister had for a husband. When I spilled out my part of the story, of how I was duped into this marriage and my utter desperation for a divorce, he fell quiet and helplessly looked at Uncle for advice. So after about an hour or so of some heavy discussions, we were all ready with our plan.

10 am: *Called up Hamid* – in my best sensual voice and asked him if he was still interested in having me back in his life. I told him that my landlords had asked me to vacate the room and I had nowhere to go. I could look for other accommodation but I still missed him. After flirting with him for some time, I asked him to meet me at a nearby coffee shop and start all over again. I had overestimated him, as all people need is a few words of love to surrender themselves.

11:00 am: *Café Al Noor.* I was shaking inside with nervousness but this was my one chance to finish it off. While I sat in a plush sofa that devoured my enormous hips, I thought of our frequent trips here and longed for the same old *kahwa* with date *mamools.* My restless eyes kept looking out for Hamid. What if he changed his mind? But not for long, as there he entered through the main door and turned some heads too – with the same crisp white *thobe* on his tall body and black leather sandals. I kept soaking in the sight of him as I knew that this was perhaps the last time I would be seeing my handsome Hamid. Yes, a part of me still loved him, but not enough to destroy my own life with this thug. The nearer he came, the more I felt his electrifying aura, mixed with our history together and the reality of the current situation. Before he could greet me, I took centre stage and started wailing and beating my chest. Soon enough, we had a crowd around us – the people who were sipping their own *kahwas* and the staff behind the counters – to witness the excitement. Hamid found it impossible to register the scene till he saw his first wife, her brother and lawyer Uncle approaching him. When I saw colour escaping his face I knew that he was resigned, there was no point fleeing from there as he was ambushed.

12 noon: *Talaq, Talaq, Talaq.* So, after an hour of melodrama, amidst accusations of mental torture from my side, some solid Punjabi abuses from his, and pressure from his family and the self-designated leaders in the café, he had no choice but to divorce me. But he promised that he would ruin me, whatever it took. He meant it.

In my mid-twenties, I was a two-time divorcee and mother of four young children. Mehrunissa's brother promised that he would get the divorce papers through soon due to his contacts in the government.

However, I had absolutely no time to accept it fully and mourn my life. I had a big event in the evening and was already running late. No time for *iddat.* Basic necessities of life come first.

4:00 pm: *Customer's house*. In the hall of this heavily decorated villa, I had ten-odd heavily made-up women, sitting around me and waiting for their turn for me to make intricate designs on their palms with the slimy olive-green henna paste in plastic cones. Tonight was *Mehendi*, followed by Ladies' *Sangeet*, for a dainty young girl in a traditional orange *sharara*. There were sounds of collective laughter whenever a joke was cracked about the groom's virility or their honeymoon plans. The atmosphere in the Pakistani household was upbeat with Indian film music playing in the background – *mehendi laga ke rakhna, doli saja ke rakhna*. A couple of times, I would notice the girl's mother shedding a tear or two and then being consoled by the family about how lucky her daughter was to be getting married into such a high-status family. I guess that is all that matters in our society. Status. Something I could never dream of having. And marriage – I had had enough of it already.

6:00 pm: *Some makeup and more*. After the henna ceremony I accompanied the girl to her room and helped her get dressed up for the next event that involved dancing and some more dancing. The pale and puny girl with long straight brown hair, all of twenty, seemed almost as nervous as I was in the café this morning, but for completely opposite reasons. I remembered my own time, not so long ago, when the thought of *suhaag raat* used to send shivers up my spine and a delicious feeling down in the pit of my stomach. I had not fully accepted that I was not married any more. But slowly the sense of loss got pronounced due to the irony of the situation – here I was, a *talaqshuda*, pretending to be rejoicing in this girl's wedding. I had no choice but to carry on as I always did with my customers but tonight I was finding it difficult to put on my happy-go-lucky act. Maybe I had a hunch that something terrible was going to happen.

8:00 pm: *Chori ka ilzaam*. When I had done my job, I couldn't help feeling proud of how I had transformed this average girl into a ravishing beauty. The girl, too, stood admiring herself in the mirror and hugged her mother who had just entered the room. Babbling about how daughters are actually someone else's *amanat*, the mother opened the bedside drawer and shrieked in shock. She started tossing the stuff out from all the other drawers and her cupboard. Her expression changed to that of sheer disgust and she turned to me, demanding her twenty thousand riyals back.

'What, madam? I don't know what you are talking about, I haven't even seen that much money in my life!' I cried helplessly.

In no time, she had called her husband, who entered with their grown-up sons. They gathered around me and I was threatened to hand over the money or else they would call the police. I was the only outsider in the room, so obviously it was me. I folded my hands and fell at their feet and pleaded with them. I had not touched or even seen the money but they refused to listen and kept calling me names. So now I was not only a *bazaaru aurat* but also a despicable thief!

These torturous moments went on for a few minutes that seemed like eternity till a thought hit me. I was innocent. What did I have to worry about if I had not done it? Suddenly I got up from the floor and stood facing the man directly. I dared him to touch me and insisted they call the police. I had done being scared and was ready for anything. The man held back nervously and asked me to pick up my stuff and leave the house right away. Maybe they were trying to ward off any *badshaguni* on this auspicious night. But I still demanded my payment of five hundred riyals on my way back home: I could not let go of my hard-earned money, after all.

10:00 pm: *Back home.* As I lay in my bed, completely drained of any energy and feeling absolutely empty from inside, I just stared and stared at the ceiling. I could not do anything but laugh uncontrollably. Allah, why? Why me? What are you punishing me for? All I wanted was to be able to support my children. Why was I cursed, what did I do, what did I do, *what did I do?* The laughter soon turned into a heavy fall of hot tears streaming from my bloodshot eyes, down my cheeks and wetting my pillow, to which I held on, thinking of my babies.

DAY TWO

7:00 am: *Phone rings.* 'Aunty, this is me, Sahiba.' I was too drowsy to understand who it was and what she was trying to say, when she continued in a shaky voice: '. . . remember last night, when my parents accused you of theft, I knew all along that it was not you. But I stood watching as I dared not open my mouth to let out the truth. Even now, only Allah knows how I have mustered up the courage to call you but please promise me you will not tell anyone.' Further, 'It was my Abbu who did it, and I saw it with my own eyes. He took it for his girlfriend, probably, I am not sure, but I cannot let Ammi know or she will die. It's a long story . . . I cannot go on, but I just called up to apologize. Please forgive us, Aunty.'

I let out a sigh of relief and thanked Allah for saving my honour. Wait, was I just called aunty by a girl nearly my age? Women.

10:00 am: *Phone rings again.* This time it was my sponsor. Though it was still a couple of months to go before my visa had to be renewed, she called me up, claiming that she needed the cash NOW. Though I had saved enough, now she had simply doubled the amount. 'But Madam, from where will I get that kind of money, I am just a beautician, not a thief . . .' I stressed the last three words to perhaps remind myself that I wasn't. She told me that times had changed, everything was getting more expensive and she knew that I had built up a very sound practice and had even stolen some of her salon's customers. That this was the least I could do for all that she had done for me. After some negotiations, she asked me to settle it with her in the evening. I was to bring my *ikama* and whatever money I had. As a usual practice, my passport was already with her.

6:00 pm: *Madam's salon.* After work, I went to meet her. I discussed my problems with her and told her how difficult I was finding it to manage, even though working like a mule. Although she was listening, I was sensing some strange, dark energy around her, as if something really bad was going to happen but I could not pinpoint exactly what. I liked and respected the woman. She seemed to be fair in her dealings; I reminded myself that she was involved in a lot of charitable causes – but why was I feeling so uncomfortable in her presence?

7:00 pm: After taking whatever money I had and finishing off our inconclusive meeting, she told me that she would drop me to my house, which I politely and anxiously declined, saying that I could walk down as it was hardly any distance. I was already feeling trapped but she sounded very firm about it. So when I sat in the back seat of her car with her two bouncers of sons on either side of me, my hands turned ice-cold. She sat in the front with her third son and the car took another route. I kept begging her to let me go but by now it was too late.

8:00 pm: *King Fahd International Airport, Al Khobar.* They dropped me off at the airport and handed me my ticket and passport. She had cancelled my visa, blacklisted me and was sending me back. Just like the night before, with folded hands I fell at her feet now and begged her to take pity on me. I had four children to feed, I had my livelihood here. But she stood motionless. All she said was that she could tolerate everything but not someone who sells her body. She told me that Hamid had told her that he had left me when he came to know of my dirty side business. Surely this mature, sensible businesswoman could not believe Hamid, could she? But she chose to, as a couple of my customers also had complained to her about me playing flirting games with their husbands. *But Madam, even if that was true, it still doesn't make me a prostitute!* But Madam did not budge. She had made up her mind. I had to leave the country and no matter what, she would never let me come back.

The drama was more intense than what had happened inside the café, just the day before. Passers-by stared at us, shocked. Some compassionate ones tried requesting Madam to give me another chance. There were a lot of exchanges in Arabic with the word '*haram*' repeated on and on. I lay down near the departure gate, crying aloud. *I don't want to go back. My children will starve. At least return my money.* But she did not listen. Moreover, I was really cursed as that day my cell phone credit had finished and I could not seek help from lawyer Uncle or Omar. But even if I tried, I am sure it would have been no use. I was an illegal immigrant and had no place in this country any more.

I stopped crying, gathered myself and my purse containing nothing but a useless cell phone and fifty riyals, went inside the terminal and bid goodbye to Saudi – a country that had given me so much, as even then I had the sense to think that one woman's inhumane act does not reflect on the entire nation. I thanked Allah at least I was to see my children again.

One benevolent Saudi policeman, who had witnessed the whole scene, came up to me and handed me a bill of five hundred riyals. I grabbed the money shamelessly as I really did need it for the taxi fare and some sweets for my children. I blessed him and went off, pledging in my mind that it was not over between her and me. And Hamid and me.

Nikalna khuld se aadam ka sunte aaye the lekin,
Bade be-aabru hokar tere kooche se hum nikley . . .

PAKISTAN

MARCH 2003:

KARACHI, PAKISTAN

*L*adies *and gentlemen, welcome to Jinnah International Airport. The local time is 3:30 am and the temperature is 24 degrees Celsius. On behalf of the Captain and the entire crew, I'd like to thank you for joining us on this trip and we are looking forward to seeing you on board again in the near future. Have a nice day.*

I woke up with a jolt with this announcement. Even now I haven't fully understood how I could manage to sleep during my entire flight from Al Khobar to Karachi. Perhaps nature took charge and put me in a deep slumber, to gather enough strength to face the coming days in my motherland. I thanked Allah for the safe journey and rose to walk towards the security, empty-handed except for my black purse that had a packet of chocolates which I bought with some of the money given by that kind policeman at the airport.

Dawn was just breaking when I reached Fatima's house. As my taxi moved through the narrow lanes of the *mohalla*, I glimpsed the clear orange-tinged sky through the arching trees and heard the sounds of birds chirping. I looked intently at the graffiti on the boundary walls of the neighbouring houses. Some Urdu *shaayeri*, some cartoons of politicians and some *ma-behen ki gaaliyan*. Not a good time to be in Pakistan, which was in a state of gloom following the debacle of its cricket team in the World Cup.

As I stood outside, knocking at the gate for almost ten minutes, I started panicking, thinking how the people inside would react. When Shahid Bhai opened the gate, he knew instinctively that something was drastically wrong and went inside to alert his wife and my children.

Soon everyone gathered in the corridor and I couldn't help noticing what a rude surprise it was for Fatima. I kept hugging my children whom I had not seen for almost two years. Sana, Suhana, Naveed and little Aftab. They all had grown up but looked very thin, or probably that's what all mothers think about their children, especially Indians and Pakistanis, whose favourite hobby is to feed them all the time.

After settling my children with the only gift I could bring, I looked at my elder sister and started weeping, hoping against hope for an iota of sympathy from her. I wanted her to hold me and say that it was all right, now I was home and they would take care of everything. Instead, she probed me with her countless questions about the truth of my story. Even though she did not really say it, the disbelief on her face implied that she too felt that I was a *do number ki aurat* as how was it possible for an uncouth creature like me to be able to send so much for the upkeep of her children? Surely she had never heard of a beautician making that much money, abroad or at home. It was perhaps futile to explain that this was precisely the reason people went *bahir*. Because it pays.

She did not believe me either when I told her that I did not intend to stay in Pakistan for long and would be gone as soon as possible. I had a business in Saudi and I was needed there. A few telephone calls later, all would be set.

I don't have to say it again, but I was and would always be a stupid, naïve woman. In retrospect, it was this very positivity in me that made me the person I am today, as no matter how hard the circumstances, I always believed that the future would be better.

But back then, it certainly did not look all that good. Everything conspired to make me feel that life was . . . well . . . a bitch.

That night I noticed my youngest baby Aftab sleeping with a piece of cloth wrapped tightly around his body. On further inspection, I realized it was my *dupatta* that I had forgotten here when I went to Saudi. Aftab used to cry so much for me that Fatima started swaddling him in my *dupatta* to calm him down. The trick worked but he continued even as a toddler. He was very restless and colicky, a very difficult child, and this was one way to soothe him down to sleep. Oh, poor Aftab, don't worry, your mother is with you now. Sleep well, my child. *La-la-la-la lori, doodh ki katori . . .*

Thankfully, my daughters Sana and Suhana turned out to be very caring towards Naveed and Aftab. They looked after the younger ones like mothers and shielded them from Fatima if the boys were being . . . well, boys. Fatima's daughters were discouraged from mingling with mine but girls are naturally very sensitive and the six children had adjusted well with each other. I, however, had no place in Fatima's heart or home. We both knew that it was only materialism that defined our relationship. And when she realized that my children and I would be freeloaders, she categorically asked me to look for options. I had Ammi's house. What about Khalu, our real father? Surely I could go somewhere? Though I knew it would be futile to even think about such a possibility, I still had to try, for Fatima's satisfaction and for the sake of my dignity.

The next morning I went to visit my Ammi. When I went there I realized that she had given the bigger portion of her house on rent and lived alone in the annexe. The poor woman was ailing herself, with no one to look after her as Omar was happily settled in Saudi and Rashid was completely indifferent. Abbu had left nothing but this house and some loans on her head which she tried repaying with her only source of income – the rent from the retirement home Abbu had built with so much love. I could not do anything but cry at this point in life where we both could offer each other nothing except prayers. She was my Ammi and it broke my heart to see her like this at the fag end of her life – completely cast aside and deserted by her two 'boys'. Life.

Khalu welcomed with me with open arms as he had no idea that I was looking for shelter. He lived with my two elder brothers, their wives and the six children between them. All of them in this shabby little cardboard box of a house. He claimed that his sons were doing well in life, one was a primary school teacher in and the other worked as an accountant in a garment factory. The sons were dutiful and docile but the control of the finances was in the hands of their wives who were themselves miserable in a joint family. Both had ganged up against Khalu and were sick of his ever-increasing medical expenses. I was in no mood to offer any sympathy as my own life sucked. And I did not want the additional burden of his never-ending sob stories as perhaps I had still not forgiven him in my heart for giving me away.

I had a long talk with Fatima. All I needed was a roof over my head for some time. I was her real sister; did she have no feelings at all for me? I promised to send her even more money the day I went back to Saudi, but for now I begged her not to throw my children and me out of her house. I knew that even if she gave in, soon she would have to confront her husband Shahid Bhai, who made his disapproval very clear. A no-nonsense man, all he was interested in was having some peace and quiet at home, which his wife had destroyed due to the presence of four additional children at home.

So Shahid Bhai became my next target. This was going to be a very dangerous game, which called for a lot of carefulness and meticulous planning.

Week one: Whenever Fatima was not around, I used to stare at Shahid Bhai and look away if he turned towards me. I had to go slow, as he was surely not interested. But I took the risk of brushing his hand lightly whenever handing a glass of water to him. He usually stepped back and pretended not to notice it.

Week two: My stare became more intense and now he had started staring back. I used to look away, at the same time congratulating myself on these little victories.

Week three: In Fatima's absence, I used to sway my hips a bit more and move sensually while sweeping the floor. Sometimes I would look straight into his eyes and smile invitingly. But this man was made of stone, as he still wouldn't take the hint, it seemed.

Week four: One night, Fatima and the girls went to the neighbours' for some function. My children were sleeping soundly and I knew that this was my chance. I made a cup of tea for Shahid Bhai and went into his room, leaving my dupatta and self-respect behind. He was taken aback at seeing me standing there, completely at his disposal. When I said that he was a no-nonsense man, I meant it, as all he did was take the cup from my hands and thank me before getting back to work on the computer. I could sense by now that my sensuality wasn't enough for him. Maybe he needed more. I went further and started making small talk about the internet and Google and how well researched I was on topics of health and beauty. That made an impact. He seemed to be really impressed with this woman who could talk about things other than '*gurbat*', their troubles, and ever-increasing grocery bills. We talked a lot and I realized that I did not have to be a bitch to my sister. As by now I did not have to do anything at all: I had won her husband's approval.

From the next day onwards, Fatima became slightly less mean and genuinely spoke about her problems. She told me that Shahid Bhai felt bad for me and did not mind my living in their house. Temporarily, of course. She suggested that I start looking for a job in Saudi and if that did not work, there were other Gulf countries. How about Muscat, where one of our distant cousins worked as an electrician? How about Bahrain, which she had heard so much about? Obviously, Shahid Bhai had influenced her to be kind towards a lone woman like me, as no matter what, I was still her sister. I knew that this sisterly affection would not last long, as Fatima's basic nature was greed and selfishness. But at least I was tension-free about Shahid Bhai. Mission accomplished.

However, I had to get back to business at any cost.

Skype. This wonder tool had entered the market that provided live video chats for free. When Shahid Bhai introduced me to this system, I had no idea that one day this was going to be very useful for me. But for now, most people had not heard of or used video calling.

Whatever free time I had, I spent on calling up my contacts in Saudi or sitting before the computer, looking for a job. The word had spread among my customers of my being deported from the country due to some illicit activities. Some gave useless advice, some promised help without meaning to, some called me names and some did not pick up my calls. Every night I would go to sleep after being disappointed again. Lawyer Uncle had taken an early retirement and gone back to his beloved India when poor Aunty suffered a stroke. So no help came from anywhere. I was basically idling away amidst the constant taunts of Fatima. When it got too much for me to bear, I sold off the gold ring Hamid had given me and shut Fatima's mouth with the money. Obviously, not for long.

Hamid made it really difficult to get our divorce legally registered but I called up his brother-in-law, the Saudi citizen, who helped me again and made sure the paperwork got completed smoothly. When I asked him for some more help, such as a job in his country, he refused, saying that he did not want any more complications in his life. Wise move.

I knew that I had to do something to survive. But the chances of a Pakistani 'unlicensed' beautician finding a job in the Gulf were close to nil. I had to get real and get out of the house to make a living. Right there in Pakistan. Certificates. Here too I was asked if I had any formal training. Even in the rundown beauty parlours in that *mohalla*, I was subjected to questions from these so-called beauty experts, underfed girls with narrow shoulders, dry damaged hair, chipped nail-polish and lots of foundation on their pimpled faces. Most took a dislike to this comparatively sophisticated and curvaceous woman who claimed to have her own business in Saudi. Yes, certificates or not, for the first time I was overqualified for the job. In all modesty, I think my problem was that I looked rich!

One morning, I saw an advertisement for beauty specialists in an 'upcoming International Unisex Salon' in one of the new malls in the city. They were hiring 'presentable and experienced young men and women who make the clients feel special'. I knew it was me. They were already interviewing and joining would be immediate.

The next morning, when I sensed a tinge of jealousy on Fatima's face when she saw me all dressed up in this salwar suit borrowed from her – a white synthetic one with brocade work, deep neck and short sleeves – I was confident about getting the job. Now Pakistan probably has some of the most stylish women in the world, specially the upper-class ladies; but I wasn't competing with them – I was pitted against these rebellious girls from middle-class families, having little formal education, but 'certified' in beauty, who wanted to do something with their lives. Just like me, except that my situation was really desperate, to say the least. And I am sure none of them had four children. So, Allah, among all the applicants, I am the neediest one.

No surprises here. I got the job, as thankfully I got interviewed by the owner himself – a freshly returned-from-Dubai man, who wanted to start a chain of salons in his home country. He had his long curly hair tied up in a ponytail, wore a neat black shirt with tight blue jeans – very appealing indeed. But to men like him. Extremely well groomed, he put me off further when I noticed his cat walk. But at least he was safe.

Seven thousand rupees a month – less than what I made over a weekend in Saudi. But this was the best I could do at that time. It would ease off some of the burden from Fatima's and Shahid Bhai's shoulders and I would get to hone my skills in something I felt I was born for.

I still believe that by blessing me with this *hunar* in my hands, Allah has made up for all the hardships and disappointments I have faced in my life. To me, my talent is sacred because I could feed my children because of this. Even after so many years, whenever I get appreciated by a customer who feels better in her body because of my treatments, could be facials, massages, hair – anything – as a practice I look up and thank my God. *Alhamdulillah.*

For the next few months my routine involved getting up at the break of dawn, watering the plants in their small garden, sweeping the corridors, preparing tea and *nashta* for the whole family, dressing up and feeding my children and then dropping them off to the nearby *madrasa*, before catching a bus to the mall where the salon was. As I could not afford to pay as before, my children had had to change their school. I would come back before dinnertime and then collapse with my tightly packed young ones in the bed, comforted by the familiar smell of mustard oil on their hair. But I was grateful that I had the strength and stamina for this hard work and even if I was subjected to the ever-increasing sarcasms from Fatima, I was happy that I got to see my family every day, a job that let me do what I loved and still have some money to contribute in the house. On Fridays, I would take my children to Ammi's house and listen to her miseries. Still, she would always treat us with her specialty – *lazeez* stuffed *keema parathas*. That was our only entertainment. As I gorged on those *parathas*, I used to thank God that I had practically no time to dwell on my own worries.

Considering my recent history, life could not have been better and as soon as I said this aloud, I knew this was not to last long. I couldn't stay here for ever. I had to find a solution as Fatima had given me some more-than-clear hints that I had to find my own place to stay. Or go back to the Gulf and start sending money as before. Or get married again.

Who would believe that a few proposals had come my way? From widowed old men with grown-up children. All decent men, who wanted to give refuge to a cast-down, abandoned woman like me. They did not mind the extra four mouths to feed that would come as dowry. All in the name of charity.

There were two main reasons that I said 'no' to all of them. One was that, by now, the word 'marriage' had begun to repel me so much that I had taken a secret oath to never ever get into this *jahannum* again and second, even if I disregarded that secret oath, none of them were rich enough to make me want to do it. Some bald lower-middle-class men in faded Pathani suits and embroidered Punjabi *jutties*, grinning with *paan*-stained teeth. Revolting.

They reminded me of Adil Chacha, except that Chacha was still handsome. Once I had a strong urge to visit him and my old house, which was just a few minutes away. I also wanted to see this woman whom the father of my four children, Wasim, had married. Sometimes, I would be left open-mouthed at the indifference of this maniac who had cried so much when I had left him. This cold-hearted *jallad* had not attempted to ever call up his own flesh and blood. Didn't he ever miss them? Did he have absolutely no duty towards his children? I wasn't entirely surprised that his second wife was still childless, even after so many years of marriage. But I was amazed at myself that I never ever asked him to share my burden, even in my hardest of times. Maybe it fed my ego to be shouldering all responsibilities alone. I am not sure. But I was sure that some things had better be left alone. For the time being. So I never visited Wasim or Adil Chacha. However, I still longed to see my youngest brother-in-law. My friend, my confidant Iqbal. I remembered how he had sparked my love of learning by bringing home books for me. And how much he had shielded me from his older brother's thrashings. I was sure that the 'good boy' must have done something with his life and be happily married by now. As I said, some things had better be left alone.

Because as usual, I had my hands full – of blow-dryers,

hair-extensions, wax strips, artificial nails – you name it. My salon was in an upmarket mall that sold almost all the brands I had seen in the Middle East. Pakistan always had some very fashionable women but some clients looked even better than the actresses from TV dramas. Though I was used to attractive women, I still felt proud thinking that the women of my country were some of the best-looking in the world, maybe as good as the Hindi film heroines. But then we all belong to the same part of the earth if you don't consider the man-made territories. This feeling is deeply imbued in me and most people who have lived abroad. That we are all one. Yes, I was turning less cynical and more philosophical. Pakistan was working. Especially now that I had made some friends in the salon, including my effeminate boss, Hasan.

Because of our common Middle-East background, he had probably taken an interest in me. He was a trusting soul who only saw good in others. Even though he had a difficult childhood, being bullied in school and unaccepted by his own family, he had turned out to be a decent, hardworking and compassionate businessman. He got along with everyone in the salon and rewarded us generously, especially after a good feedback from a customer. All of us waited our turn to pamper him with facials, massages and pedicures. I had poured my heart out to this tender person who always listened graciously. He promised that one day he would help me achieve my dreams – and yes, I believed him.

Hasan proved himself. He told me that the first step was to go in for some formal training. I needed those certificates on my resume. Surely I did not want to settle down in Pakistan and be content with this meagre income? *I was something else – ambitious, talented, smart. I had the X factor, whatever it meant. I deserved a real career, I deserved respect. And my children – they deserved the best education money could buy.* So, all charged up with this motivating speech, I rose up, looked into his eyes and said: 'Yes, boss, in the name of my children and the talent Allah has bestowed in my hands, I will do it.'

But I had no idea what I was supposed to do. His eyes went to the computer on the receptionist's table and he asked me to do some relevant research on the internet. I had to look for and make a list of the top ten beauty certifications in the world and then bring the list down to the top three least expensive that could be done online or preferably in the city. So after spending half a day on this 'research project', I submitted the report to my boss. Yes, Google had not let me down and I ended up signing up for three courses – in 'Relaxation Massages', 'Invigorating Facials' and 'Eyelash Perming and Tinting'! Hasan looked as excited as me and promised to pay for these courses, which he felt would 'take my career to the next level'. I was happier because I got a 15 per cent discount since I had purchased three courses from that popular website. Oh, to be a student again.

However, it was the beginning of the end at Fatima's house; she had become openly blunt about her disapproval of having us in her house. My seven thousand were just not enough to feed my hungry mongrels. She did not want a dishonourable woman spoiling the atmosphere of her home, she had no privacy, she did not want the responsibility any more. She was perhaps sick of seeing us all in her house. It was difficult for me to take the insults any more. Sometimes, she would shout at me so much that Shahid Bhai would come to my rescue, which used to enrage her even more. I was taking it all as I had no place to go. One family by birth and one by adoption – and still I was all alone.

This went on for a few months and, as always, work became my refuge. The salon was growing and I got my first pay hike of two thousand rupees. Still not enough to move out and provide for my family, unless I took a room on rent, but Ammi always said that it was better I got humiliated within four walls, rather than being exposed outside. Anyway, she was sure that no regular family would give out a room to a single woman with four children. I could move in with her but those days Rashid had started staying with his mother off and on so there was no place for all of us. I also noticed that she no longer had that gold bangle on her – her one possession, Abbu's *aakhri nishaani*. Rashid had made her sell it as he needed the money for a motorcycle. Who was I counting on? I decided that there was no way out except *bahir*. Till then all I had to do was to swallow my pride in Fatima's house.

One day, I saw Hasan talking to someone on Skype – the wonder chat software that I was talking about. When I entered his chamber, he turned his laptop around and introduced me to his uncle in Bahrain. After exchanging pleasantries, I left to get on with my job. Little did I know that this chance encounter with someone far, far away would lead to my life changing again. And this time forever.

'What are you talking about, Hasan? I don't understand. How is it even possible?' Shaking violently, I blurted these words when Hasan came to talk to me the next day. He told me that his uncle, the one he was chatting with, had enquired about me as he was looking for a personal secretary. Hasan had recommended me, a beautician with absolutely no office experience and three random certifications in massage, facials and eyelashes, to join his company in Bahrain! I was speechless but Hasan went on and on about how enterprising I was and would be able to learn quickly. Uncle was a renowned businessman in Bahrain and had hundreds of people working in his company. Hasan had told my story to him and he wanted to help out. Even the money wasn't bad. I would be given accommodation, air tickets, visa, and after a probation period of three months, if the management approved, I could even call my children on 'family status'. 'But why me, Hasan, surely he could get someone more qualified from Bahrain itself?' I asked. Hasan replied with a straight face, 'Because, Sawera darling, my uncle is a good man, and at whatever cost, this is your one big chance in life that you cannot blow away.' At whatever cost.

BAHRAIN

AUGUST 2005:

BAHRAIN INTERNATIONAL AIRPORT

'**I**s it just me or is the world suddenly a happy place?' I thought to myself when I said goodbye to the cabin crew standing at the exit of this packed flight from Karachi, full of Pakistanis – young, old, rich, poor, men, women and children – all excited at reaching this small island. Some had been living here for decades while others were newcomers like me. But the air had a feel of belongingness about it – something like when you are home.

As I passed the security and baggage claim, I noticed that everyone was smiling at me. Was my *abaya* too tight or was I looking like a lost case? I realized quickly that most people were just smiling away at each other – for no particular reason. Yes, in Saudi too I had noticed that westerners smiled on eye contact but here it didn't matter where they were from.

I came out and saw him. A tall figure with greying hair, rimless glasses, a black designer suit and an aura that distinguished him from all others. People kept turning their heads to get a glimpse of this gentleman who looked straight out of those popular TV soaps. Oh yes – a cross between my favourite Noman Ijaz and the evergreen Indian actor Anil Kapoor. As soon as our eyes met, a current ran down my body – this man, he who gave me this job, he who brought me to this 'happy place', he who would make all my problems go away, my *farishta* – finally I had met him. Adnan Uncle.

In the back seat of his shiny black car, I felt mesmerized. He was busy with the keys of what looked like a brand-new phone and would talk to his driver from time to time. I could not decide what was a better sight – the wide flyovers on the blue Arabian Sea or this man sitting in the front seat. I kept looking out through the window and made a mental note to soon visit the enormous structure with the biggest dome I had ever seen in my life – the Grand Mosque we passed on our way to Juffair.

Juffair. Uncle told me that originally a village, it was now part of the suburban expansion of the city and included reclaimed land from the sea that had extended Bahrain's coastline. I had no clue what he was talking about but I was soaking in each word that escaped his mouth like it was *shaayeri*. I saw construction happening everywhere and Uncle told me that in a few years this would become the most sought-after place in Bahrain. Of course, he knew as he was in the real-estate business himself. Then he gave me an account of the hotels, apartment blocks and land he owned in the Gulf and how he was now expanding his business in Bahrain. Well, for now it was too much information for a *ganwaar* like me and I realized that no matter how many hours one spent on Google, it could never replace real education.

Thankfully I realized we had reached our destination when I noticed the car stopping near this new building which seemed almost vacant. As we went into the lift, he started off again about this being his latest project and he was hoping that the building would fill up with tenants soon and then he cursed the competition from other builders. My head felt like it was going to burst and my jaw was aching owing to my fake smiles. Oh God, is this another mess I have landed myself in? What was I thinking when I packed up my bags to come to Bahrain without doing an 'online certification' in 'Real Estate' and then wondered if such a certification even existed! Probably Hasan had motivated me just too much for my own good.

We went inside what is called a studio apartment. Basically one main room that has a bed, a sofa set, a small kitchenette and an 'en suite' bathroom. Well, not too different from our small unplanned houses in Pakistan, except that this looked 'high class'. He gave me a mobile phone and left, saying that he would come later, after I had had some rest.

As I looked around my new home, I noticed how self-contained this space was – a wall-mounted flat-screen TV, a large fridge, a microwave, a washing machine, a bathtub – it had everything. It was heaven. Being a beautician, I had already seen much bigger and more decorated houses in Saudi, but none belonged to me. But this one, I had earned myself. Finally, *apna ghar.*

After having a hot shower – a typical problem of the Gulf – in summer the water from the 'cold water' taps is warmer than the water from the geyser – I collapsed on the sofa and my mind went back to that fateful day in Hasan's office two months back and my unforgettable journey since then.

SOME DAYS AGO IN PAKISTAN

'*Pagal ho gayee hai kya?*' Fatima roared at me as if I had just confessed about a secret plan to kill someone. She did not believe it when I told her about my chance 'hello-hi' on Skype with a successful Pakistani businessman in Bahrain who happened to be my boss's *Tayajaan* and who had offered me a job. Shahid Bhai did not believe it, either. Neither did I.

But when Hasan handed over an appointment letter to me the next day, I couldn't help crying. My prayers had been answered. I could now pay for my children's upkeep and even call them to me, if all went well. After ages, I would have some money in my hands. I could buy new clothes for my children. Toys too. Maybe I could even get a new bangle for Ammi.

Even though I was a nervous wreck, I was still practical enough to try clearing my numerous doubts with Hasan. He gave me the confidence to go ahead and stop thinking so much. His uncle was a prominent figure in the family, someone everyone looked up to. Uncle had financially helped Hasan set up his salon. He even donated to various charities. Do I have to say that it didn't really make me feel any better?

But I had to take this chance as there was no way that I could live even a day more in Fatima's house. Things were really messy between us now, with her blaming me and my children for their bad luck. *Come on Fatima, just because your husband didn't get you a new gold chain this Eid, you can't call it bad luck!* But that thankless woman expected me to do all the housework and still contribute financially. The last straw that broke my back was her accusation of me wanting to grab her husband. What was she talking about, me and Shahid Bhai? Seriously? OK, I admit that she was a little bit right but that was long back and I had moved on.

Meanwhile, there were a lot of worries. I was going to an absolutely new country. I had no contacts whatsoever there. I had zero knowledge of office work. My new boss had not even interviewed me before sending out an appointment letter. What if I got kicked out from Bahrain too? My head was spinning out of control and I couldn't stop these thoughts from taking over my mind but then I was Sawera. The emotional, impulsive one, who was considered lucky when she was born. The one who let her heart rule her head. I was sure that my time had come and whatever happened, it could not be as bad as my past.

My children cried for hours when I broke this news to them. They felt again betrayed by their mother and no matter how much I tried to reassure them, they had stopped trusting me. They kept begging me not to go, promising to never trouble Fatima Aunty, never make a noise when Shahid Uncle slept, never ask for a new toy, study every day and never fall sick too. I kept promising to call them as soon as I could but they knew. They just did.

The coming days were not so sad as Adnan Uncle had transferred some money for my new passport and some necessary paper work. It was enough to pay for all the formalities and a lot extra to buy new clothes and toys for my children. I still cannot forget the look on their innocent faces when I laid down the goodies on the bed. *Salwar* suits for the twins and *sherwanis* for my little lads, who picked up the toy truck and motorcycle and went outside to play. Sana, merely eight or nine years old, who was still in the room, looked at all the 'things' and asked me, 'Ammi, does this mean you are really going?' I hugged my daughters and we all cried together. Was this what I called 'not so sad'?

BACK TO THE STUDIO IN BAHRAIN

Startled by the sound of the door opening, I woke up, rubbing my wet eyes. It was late evening. I saw this tall silhouette switching on the lights. 'Oh, Adnan Uncle, it's you!' I cursed myself for forgetting to lock the door but soon realized he had the spare keys, which he had used to enter my house. With my heart pounding, I nervously asked him to sit and tried looking for the kettle to prepare a cup of tea for him. He told me to just sit down as all he wanted was to talk. His eyes grew softer and he started with his favourite topic, real estate – words I had started to dread by now. Sensing my uneasiness, he soon changed the subject. He enquired about me, my children and what my goals in life were. 'Honestly, Uncle . . . I have not really thought about it . . . I do know what I want but perhaps I am not so good at expressing myself,' I replied anxiously, while praying in my heart that he wouldn't decide to send me back due to my lack of 'communication skills'.

He laughed out aloud and told me that actually he liked people who were honest and straightforward. And when he saw me on Skype the other day, he knew that I was the one. I was surprised and relieved, thinking that there are more people in this world who act on impulse. I felt pride in the thought that we both shared this same quality. I just hoped he would not regret his decision of calling me to Bahrain.

I don't know when exactly he moved closer and took my shaky hand in his. I was taken aback at the guts of this old man; all right, he was rich, handsome and successful but I wasn't just some piece of trash lying on the road, either.

I rose from the sofa and politely asked him to leave. He laughed again. What was I thinking? Why was I here? Did I really think he needed a personal secretary? All he wanted was someone to comfort him, to look after him when he came back from a hard day at work, to listen to him, to sleep with him.

'Adnan Uncle, why me? I am sure with your kind of stature and money, you could find someone from here, someone more glamorous, sensuous and more . . . professional?'

'I am a traditional man, Sawera, I like *shareef, khandaani* women . . . not those pencil-thin models in miniskirts and high heels loitering around on near these five-star hotels at night. Of course, I can get any woman I want but I want you and no one else. Secondly, you will not call me Uncle from now on.'

Ya Khuda! Shareef, khandaani women don't fall into muck like this, but in my heart I loved the sound of the word *khandaani*, which someone had called me probably the first time in my life. I don't remember anything else except the next few minutes all I did was cry and curse my pitiful life, till he got up to leave. The gentleman promised me that he would never force himself on me and would touch me only when I was ready.

As soon as he left, I called up my ex-boss and screamed into my cell phone: 'Hasan, you don't know what you have done. Your uncle is not a respectable man, he doesn't want a secretary, he needs someone to fuck! Get me out of here, I want to come back! *Ya* Allah, *utha le mujhe . . .*' Hasan asked me to calm down before continuing in a firm, manly voice – totally unlike him – 'Sawera, sweetheart, what did you think, a *jahil* woman like you was really called to a foreign country to work in an office? I thought you understood the hidden intentions of my uncle. And you are so wrong. He *is* an honourable, well-respected person. All right, he has had some random girlfriends but nobody is perfect, all he wants is some love. Surely you could do that much for him?'

'Girlfriend? Girlfriend? Have you gone mad, Hasan, you pimp, he wants a mistress, a *rakhael!*' I shouted. 'Grow up, Sawera, I was just trying to make you feel better about a situation that you, yourself, asked for. You wanted to go abroad, you wanted to earn more money, you wanted a better life for your children, didn't you? And now you are getting it all, and you want to blow it away. Talk about being ungrateful.'

Before I could react, he disconnected the call. He never did answer my calls since then.

As I looked down from the balcony on this top floor, I was enveloped in a strong feeling of sheer hatred and envy for the people down there: men and women walking or driving their new cars on the road, easy-going and carefree, completely oblivious to the plight of women like me – alone, desperate and poor. Yet I couldn't help noticing that this did not look like a strict, stuck-up, conservative place. Passers-by were dressed up in T-shirts and shorts, even women. Some were even smoking. Some were in gym wear and jogging. The atmosphere was very 'cool' indeed, for the lack of a better word.

What could I do, should I continue crying or try to look for some food to eat? As I was very hungry by now.

I went down into a brightness I had never seen before. The Al Shabab Road, popularly known as the Food Street: on either side this commercial avenue has all the restaurants and fast-food joints in the world. McDonald's, Starbucks, Nando's, Burger King, Chilli's, you name it. All the outlets that I had visited in Saudi on rare occasions. But much, much more. A gang of motorcycles passed by and shook the ground with their loud but synchronized sound. I noticed some couples walking by, holding hands. An old white man with a very young oriental woman, a young local boy with a middle-aged white woman. Tall black men with short brown girls. Chaotic but still blending seamlessly in the soothing harmony of the place. Some were in groups – all nationalities, all cultures, completely accepting and non-judgemental. Filipinos, Asians, Americans and, of course, Arabs – all having a good time at almost midnight but there were no signs of retirement on this busy, jovial, adventurous road where anything could happen over . . . well, a chicken burger.

As I walked home, holding a brown paper bag with a Big Mac, some changed feelings came over me. I had started to like this country already, which welcomed everyone. Adnan Saab seemed like a decent person, despite his intentions. I needed the money. Perhaps I could request him to let me work somewhere else? I was sure that there were many beauty salons that could hire me, especially with my 'international' experience.

The next evening when I asked him, he laughed. What was I

thinking? I guess I had still not realized the delicacy of the situation. I was brought to Bahrain on his visa. I was living in a house given by him. He owned me and I was going to be his keep and nothing else.

'All right, Adnan Saab, I will live in this house. I will wait for you to come back to me every evening. In return you will pay me the salary as in the contract. I will not go out searching for another job. I will comfort you, I will listen to you, I will honour you. And I promise to be faithful. But you have to fulfil your part of the promise too. That you will not touch me till I am ready.'

Oh, the quirks of the super-rich! I seemed to have turned him on even more with my statements about faithfulness and honour. He said he was proud of choosing me to be his companion in bed as he wasn't the type to sleep with just anybody. His standards were very high, after all. He knew that I was a woman of substance, again impressing me all over again with this wonderful title! I had begun to like this man who gave this kind of respect to women, including a whore like me.

Now, don't get me wrong. I was in a country where prostitution or illicit sex is strictly forbidden and is a punishable offence. The country is open but still conventional. When I questioned Adnan Saab about it, he told me that what he was doing wasn't completely legal but obviously the only person who could prove that was me and he knew I wouldn't as we were both equally responsible. He assured me that I was not a prostitute, I was in fact his companion and he felt responsible for my well-being. He was leaving for London for two weeks and commanded me to be a 'good girl' and not loiter around here and there. He gave me the number of his driver in case of an emergency and some money for bare necessities. Some money – as much as my three months' salary in Pakistan.

So this was my first day as an official mistress. I woke up, went down to the restaurant called Dome. It was my first time. Of having 'The Big Breakfast' comprising grilled beef bacon, toast and hash browns. Then I came up to my room and watched TV before dozing off till evening. Got up with rumbling sounds coming from my stomach and headed down again in hunt of food. All these years the best I knew about fine dining was Pizza Hut but now I was progressing in life by having that exotic coffee-flavoured dessert in Café Italiana. When I asked the waiter what the word Tiramisu meant, he told me it is 'Pick me up'. I laughed at the thought of having something in common with a sweet dish!

As I walked around the street, stuffed with food, studying those jolly faces, I felt nauseated. I couldn't eat more that day but promised myself that I would plan my meals more carefully. But not before grabbing a Chicken Shawarma before calling it a day. Just in case.

Next day my breakfast was a *naan* with hummus, lunch was *seekh kebab* and dinner was just a small Margarita. Sorry, it wasn't that small, actually.

So my next few days were spent exploring each and every eatery in Juffair. This was the first time in my life I could afford to eat whatever I wanted. Even though I would feel guilty for enjoying this kind of a variety while my children were probably having the usual *dal-chawal*, I still couldn't help rejoicing in the contentment good food could provide. For a starving tigress like me, who devoured everything on her plate, everything was 'bloody good'. Mind you, you have to actually experience Middle-Eastern hospitality to believe it – the portions are XXXL! Maybe I was making up for all the times in my life when I craved for something 'different' to eat, but couldn't. I actually started feeling nice. So the famous poet who said *After a good dinner one can forgive anybody, even one's own relatives*, was almost right.

But good times don't last long, especially in cursed lives such as mine. When I saw the look on Adnan Saab's face when he came back from UK, I knew that something was very wrong. Maybe the police found out about me or was it his wife? I didn't even know if he had one, so I just stood there, with a hand on my hip, waiting for him to tell me.

'Sawera, what have you done to yourself? You look so . . . puffed up!' he said unbelievingly.

'Oh, yes, Adnan Saab, I might have put on some kilos here and there, you know – family tendency,' I justified.

'Well, I am sorry but this is not what I bargained for. I knew that you were a voluptuous woman but now you are turning into a beast. You need to stop right now,' Adnan Saab said very firmly.

Oh, the humiliation! I could not do anything except feel ashamed standing in front of this man, who had heavily invested in me. Yes, I was getting the 'hang' of his vocabulary, too.

He ordered me to stop going down to my favourite street, and next day, registered me with a company that delivered 'wholesome, nutritious, low-calorie food'. I was then enrolled in a nearby gym and had a personal trainer whose job was to make me 'fitter, leaner and healthier'! Not to forget this beautician who was hired to come over twice a week and did to me what I did unto others all my life! Karma.

'Oh, this is life,' I thought to myself as I drifted into deep relaxation, feeling the smooth pressure of these oily hands that were gliding on my aching back. My body, completely worn out with years of 'treating' others, had been craving for this day when somebody else would work me up, pamper me and listen to what I had to say and not the other way round. Those stressful years of being a therapist to my customers had left me with a heavy heart so when I got a chance to speak my mind, much to the amusement of this Indian beautician, there was no stopping me. As I babbled about my children, my Ammi and lack of love in my life, I fell asleep.

When I woke up, I noticed I was all alone in the studio, which was scary. I was so used to the commotion of Fatima's house and the salon in Pakistan that this silence was in fact deafening. I put my hands over my ears and went down, even though Adnan Saab had forbidden me to loiter around here and there. But I wasn't going down to eat, there were better things to do – such as looking at other people eating food.

My evenings were spent waiting for Adnan Saab to come home. Most days he did. Besides 'real' topics like children, money and the latest gadgets in the market, he also talked about love, spirituality and lessons that life teaches you. I learnt that he was married and divorced twice. His ex-wives were in Pakistan and he had six children in all – aged from twenty-four to seven. The older children were studying in prestigious colleges in the UK and the younger ones were in school in Pakistan. His first wife left him as he had no time for her while he was busy building up his business in the Gulf. The second wife, whom he loved the most in the world, he left when he came to know about her romance with a young employee of his. He had loved and lost twice and had decided that no matter what, he would never ever get married again. He didn't have to, actually, as since his second divorce, he had got into relationships with stunning women who were always at his disposal and never asked questions. All they needed was his money. He spoke about his mistresses more fondly than he did about his wives and went on and on about their beauty and sensuousness. His last one was a belly dancer in one of the hotels in the city and that was where he had met her – a ravishing beauty from Russia, white as a dove, with wavy golden hair, blue eyes and a little waist that used to flutter rhythmically when he made love to her. He had come close to falling in love when she disappeared – from the hotel and from his life. He later heard that she had got married to her lover, a decent man working as a teacher in a school. That is when he realised that money is not everything and no amount could guarantee a woman's loyalty. Other things such as respect, care and communication counted too. Perhaps this was why he used to talk to me a lot. Perhaps he had no one else. Despite having a big family. Just like me.

So for a long time, all we did was talk.

That's how most of my initial days in Bahrain were. Though it took me a long time to adjust to a life of having 'nothing to do', soon I started enjoying the freedom, the aloofness and those countless hours with the TV as well as the treadmill.

I was over that craze for food too and was gymming my way to the body Adnan Saab had 'bargained for'. Within a couple of months, I was a new Sawera. From a curvy, soft woman with a double chin, a big bust and bigger butt, I metamorphosed into this Bipasha Basu lookalike – taut skin, well-defined broad shoulders, washboard abs, a tight butt – a total knockout. Well . . . I am just trying to sound dramatic there. Honestly, all I had become was a slimmer version of myself, as no matter how much weight you lose, the person you are will never change.

Adnan Saab seemed very pleased indeed, now he had a woman he could flaunt in his social circles. So when he asked me to accompany him to a party, I was nervous as hell. How could I go, I couldn't speak English properly, I didn't know anybody, I wouldn't know what to talk about. And the biggest problem of womankind. Of having nothing to wear.

The next day we went shopping to Al Seef Mall. Well, it wasn't the first time I was visiting one as Saudi has even larger malls with the best and most luxurious brands in the world. But honestly, this was going to be the first time that I would *buy* something from there, and that too for myself – not something I needed but something I just . . . fancied.

Jeans from Marks and Spencer, tops from Zara, dresses from Mango, stilettoes from Paris Hilton, accessories from Swarovski, makeup from Chanel. And finally a Louis Vuitton – just like the one I had drooled over in the Saudi airport. So whoever said that money couldn't buy happiness, was simply . . . well . . . lying.

And when Adnan Saab said that money could not guarantee a woman's love, he was lying too. As that night I let him touch me.

All these weeks of just 'talking' had further intensified the fire burning inside us. Now that I thought about it, these years of living a sexless life were now beginning to drive me crazy. And, of course, I had the opportunity to do it, too. With this gorgeous man. Rich and powerful. Ethical enough to not touch me all this while and still paying for it. What more could I ask for?

That night I realised that there is a big difference in the way the poor and the rich make love. The rich just know. They like to spend a long time in teasing and foreplay before getting down to the final act. They are passionate and actually considerate of the other person. They move slow but move confidently. Just like the graceful leopard, eying its prey before it pounces to kill. And they love to experiment, too. Sometimes we would indulge in a bit of 'role play' where I used to pretend to be an intellectual, like a college professor or a journalist, and it would make him go weak in the knees.

So we did it all. We did it everywhere. In the bathtub with candles around it making ruby lights in the glasses of red wine, in the kitchen while I cooked his favourite mutton *rogan josh* in a red chiffon saree and no blouse, on the terrace of one of his penthouses; under a blanket of stars in a dark sky, on the brown leather sofa while watching porn, on the handmade silk carpet from Turkey – everywhere and all the time. Whenever he was with me that was all we did. The so-called 'communication' had disappeared with the frequent dust storms of the Gulf.

Back home, my children were being looked after well by Fatima. Of course, now I was in a position to shut Fatima's mouth tightly with more money than she had ever seen in her life. I didn't know how much she would spend on my children but I wasn't very worried, as at least my children were not homeless. They joined their old school and seemed happier whenever I spoke to them. But every time they reminded me of the promise I made to them when I left for Bahrain. A promise to bring them here. A promise that their mother could no longer keep.

This mother had now changed into a slut and not just any slut – I belonged to Adnan Saab, one of the most influential, distinguished and well-known faces of the elite class. I had to live up to his standards and be his escort for those exclusive parties in five-star hotels which I had only heard of, till now. I couldn't stop thinking about what the wives of his other friends would think if they saw him with me. What I didn't know was those exclusive parties were completely private, if not secret. So this small group of ridiculously wealthy businessmen and high-flying executives in their fifties and sixties were accompanied by these scintillating young white women in little black dresses or glistening evening gowns, who initially gave me a really bad complex. Surely they were not anybody's wives. That was the only saving grace – it didn't matter if they spoke English with an accent or looked like international models – we were all in the same boat. So instead of feeling threatened by them, I decided to learn from them – their mannerisms, the way they dressed, their subdued makeup and how they moved their bodies confidently and gracefully. There was an unspoken understanding between the men – no touching another man's property and no offers to swap. Like I said, they were the so-called distinguished gentlemen. Who were doing something not completely legal. Who probably had trusting wives at home. And these ladies – they were not college professors themselves, so what was I getting a complex about?

I tried to make the most of my time spent with Adnan Saab. He introduced me to some greatest Urdu poets like Ghalib, Gulzaar saab and Firaq. I also grew interested in learning about Adnan Saab's business, travels and the game he played on weekends – golf. My vocabulary now extended to words like *marketing strategy, competitiveness, Milan, Tokyo, birdie* and *eighteen-hole-round*. I was now able to understand a lot of what he and his friends spoke about at parties. I did not want to be a sex object any more, I wanted respect. From Adnan Saab, his friends and even those pretty ladies with the fake smiles and fake boobs. If only it was that easy.

This was my life in the first year in Bahrain. I was on a roller-coaster ride that didn't seem to stop. After a while, my 'nothing-to-do' phase wasn't working any more. There were times I felt extremely lonely and counted each minute till Adnan Saab entered the house, while there were times I felt sick of being in bed with him, especially as a conclusion to those 'socialite evenings'. Once my daughter called me from Pakistan and asked what exactly a secretary did. There was a competition in her school and children were asked to prepare a speech on their parent's 'occupation'. After helping her out with information downloaded from Google I started feeling stricken at the thought of my real job . . . This feeling got worse with time. Whenever I would walk down the street, I would imagine people staring at me, laughing behind my back, whispering about me, calling me names and pitying my poor children, whose mother was a tart in another country.

Yet to me, Adnan Saab was still my *farishta*, someone who had brought me to this country and was providing for my children. Yes, I was used. But so was he. I needed him and he needed me. So I made the big mistake. Because that evening, I felt even the building watchman smiling at me sarcastically as if he knew what I did for a living. And I could not continue living like this any more.

When he heard what I suggested, he looked at me with shock before bursting into laughter, embarrassing me even further. 'Adnan Saab, why are you laughing? I am only asking you to marry me.' I blushed. But Adnan Saab just laughed and laughed even more. And then I understood. I had just become a big joke for him and nothing else.

'Oh, Sawera, I was so right about you. You really are an innocent child,' he said, controlling his laughter. Further, 'You want to marry Adnan Khan? Do you know who I am? I am one of the richest Asians in the Gulf, I have businesses spreading across the Middle East and Europe, I have hundreds of people working for me, I have built hospitals, roads, schools in Pakistan, I have plans on joining politics once I go back to my home country. I command respect. People are in awe of me. And I will marry *you*?'

'Yes, Adnan Saab, if you could sleep with me, then why not? You wouldn't just sleep with anybody. Why, you could have any woman you wanted, but you chose me to sleep with, why? Because, like you said, I am a *shareef, khandaani* woman.'

My attempt to sell myself to him was proving futile, as he just rolled his eyes and looked away. When I probed him further all he said was, 'Let's just talk about something else, Sawera. Do you want to go to the Ritz?'

That night, we did not have sex. He did not come over either, for many days thereafter. He stopped answering my calls. The loneliness was eating me up from inside. I would not even call up my children frequently as I couldn't face their never-ending questions any more. I would walk aimlessly on the streets of Juffair, disgusted at the happiness around me. I would return home late evenings and dread sleeping alone at night. This is when I got into the habit of sleeping with the lights on, along with the sounds of Hindi film songs playing on the TV.

Adnan Saab did not really approve of my going out of the house or talking to strangers. If I needed something I could just call up the cold-store boy who would leave the stuff outside my door and vanish after ringing the bell. His office settled those bills. My one contact with the outside world was the Indian beautician who used to come over for my regular maintenance. I had to make sure my skin was flawless, hair soft and silky, nails manicured and the whole body waxed at all times. Being a keep to a wealthy man wasn't an easy job, after all. And another contact was this ever-smiling Bangladeshi delivery man. Don't get me wrong, I am not talking about Pizza Hut. As even though I wasn't fat any more, I still wasn't allowed to eat anything except diet food. So every morning, I got a 'home delivery' of a colourful carton containing my five meals for the day. Typically, an apple in the morning, a small chicken sandwich for lunch, a sugar-free cookie for a snack, green salad and a mushroom soup for dinner – all within 1200 calories! The price you have to pay for a sedentary lifestyle. Sometimes I wondered if I had been better off working my butt off in the salon in Saudi and Pakistan. At least I could enjoy my *dal-chawal* with a spoonful of *desi ghee*, for heaven's sake.

So when Adnan Saab finally came over, two weeks after the night when I 'proposed' to him, I was ready with my decision. Just the way I was during Hamid's time.

When he tried touching me, I moved further away. He asked if I was feeling all right. I wasn't. As this was going to be the most important night in my life.

'Adnan Saab, when I saw you on Skype the first time, I had no idea that you would one day become the most important part of my life. I was a twice-divorced woman, working day and night to provide for my children . . . I, who had a dream of going abroad to give the best life possible to them. I was not looking for love as I had stopped believing in it. But then I met you. A man of honour. Different from all others. Successful, yet humble. Knowledgeable and a thorough gentleman. My awe had turned into respect and now this respect has turned into love, a love stronger than I have ever experienced. But I have my self-respect too and even if I have fallen in my own eyes, I haven't fallen so deep as to continue with this life of complete *zillat*. In other words, I will not let you touch me from now on. If you still want to sleep with me, marry me. If you can't, please send me back."

Adnan Saab looked at me thoughtfully. I was hoping for a dramatic act of him putting his hand in his pocket and taking out a ring for me. Of course, who could resist a *shareef, khandaani* woman who made love like a pro?

'Sawera, you really do have a deluded vision of yourself. I will ask my agent to book your tickets. When do you want to go?"

So all men are not bastards. Adnan Saab wasn't Hamid. But Sawera was Sawera – stupid and naïve. As always.

So this 'important' night of my life turned out to be nothing but a big flop.

Need I say I backed off and that it was the last time I played that trick on him? Unfortunately, I did not have a 'plan B' as yet.

The solution came in the form of that Indian beautician the next day. Even though we hardly talked, as I did not want to distract myself from enjoying my massages, I confided in her. She listened, trying not to sound amused at my story. I had not realized that she knew. I didn't have to tell her that. Of course, I was a prostitute. Kind person that she was, she did not judge me. Rekha – that was her name – told me she had heard similar stories many times.

Most are not high class like me; some even work as housemaids; but there are countless women in the Gulf, coming from not-so-rich countries, who have to do this to fulfil their responsibilities back home. It is not legal at all and some get caught. Some are sent back home while others rot in jail. But except for a handful, professional call girls, most do not have a choice.

She asked me why I was doing this, I seemed to be educated and from a good family. Why couldn't I just get out and look for work? Bahrain was an open country with good people. They could help out if I tried.

I told her that Adnan Saab would never allow me, unless . . . unless I did it without him knowing. And that is when this idea was born, yet again.

Door-to-door servicing. 'Dear Ladies, Professional beautician experienced in hair, nails and massage available at your service during morning and afternoon hours. Cheap and best. Juffair only. Contact 394922.' I wrote this down in capitals with a red marker and put up this sheet of paper on the notice board of a nearby supermarket, next to an advertisement for a second-hand car and a picture of a missing pet – an old Pomeranian bitch that was still more wanted than I was.

Now all I had to do was wait, and sure enough, calls started coming. By now, Rekha had warned me that I had to be careful not to entertain calls from men and secondly, I had to also make sure that the ladies should be from the same area so I could just walk down. Gradually the plan was to expand my business to other localities as well but for now I had to be very discreet. Slow and steady.

I paid Rekha to buy some salon supplies for me, which I had to keep hidden from Adnan Saab. If everything went well, I could probably save enough money to break away from him and get another visa to work in this amazing country.

Does this imply that I did not mean it when I said that I loved him? Maybe, as I am not sure if I believed in love any more.

But we were happy with each other. I stopped talking about marriage and started feeling comfortable being his partner in bed. No expectations. Just a good time over some interesting 'communication' that was gradually returning into our routine.

Still, I was happier when I worked. Real work. As in waxing, threading and makeup. The two or three-odd customers I saw during the first half of the day kept me going for the second half. I used to get up in the morning with a smile on my face, thinking about the appointments lined up. Ladies who were waiting for me in their homes. Who trusted me to make them look better. They believed me when I told them that I was all alone in Bahrain and doing this to support my four children in Pakistan. Almost true. But it also won a lot of sympathy for me. Respect too. *Shukran Allah*, for letting me fulfil my calling. And showing me the way.

Everything was going fine. I was saving up whatever money I made for a new visa I would need eventually. Adnan Saab was dutifully sending thirty thousand rupees to Pakistan for the upkeep of my children. Since food was delivered at home and all my other necessities were taken care of, all I got from him was a little 'pocket money' for my personal expenses. Most of it went into buying new items for my business that Adnan Saab had no idea about.

A few more months passed like this till it was time to renew my visa that typically expires in two years. I was about to discuss with him the possibility of me looking for another sponsor or a new job in a salon, when a call came from Pakistan.

'Rashid, *khairiyat*? What are you saying . . . what happened to Ammi . . . yes, I am coming . . . yes, as soon as possible . . .'

As I disconnected the phone, I looked at Adnan Saab helplessly and collapsed in his arms. I begged him to send me back and promised to return soon. I had to.

JUNE 2007:

KARACHI, PAKISTAN

This time, I could not sleep a wink during my flight to Karachi. No, it wasn't because of my Ammi – the plane that was flying through turbulence such as I had never experienced before. I was certain that this would be my last day alive and this thought made me both nervous and relieved. Maybe it was better that I died but this was not the first time I had wanted to die. The thought of my innocent children held me back from committing suicide at least two times in my life.

However, when the delayed flight landed amidst thunderstorms, we all looked up to thank Allah for bringing us to our home-country safely. However, we didn't know what was really going to hit Karachi. Soon, it went into a state of destruction with the torrential rainstorms of Sindh. Cyclone Yemyin brought floods and knocked down trees and power lines, killing hundreds and injuring even more, permanently affecting the lives of more than a million people in the country.

When I witnessed the impact of nature's fury, my frivolous life in Bahrain, my ailing Ammi and my deserted children no longer seemed like a heavy load. Thank you, Allah, as I was still alive and had the courage to live on and provide for my family.

But life goes on. Even amidst the storms, Fatima and my children could not contain their excitement when they saw me, especially when they understood that this time I did not come empty-handed. Even though I came in a hurry, I still had time for some shopping from the duty free at Bahrain Airport. For the children, it was the usual Kit Kat, Milka and Galaxy chocolates. But Fatima celebrated with her items, which actually Adnan Saab had bought for his favourite keep –a traditional silk *jalebia*, a pack of Maybelline lipsticks, a Fendi clutch . . . what more could this greedy woman ever hope for in her life? I proudly gifted a mobile phone, a Blackberry, no less, to Shahid Bhai. Everyone applauded and did not notice that he himself did not feel too pleased with this electronic marvel. So what if it wasn't totally new but Adnan Saab had hardly used it before getting the new version for himself. But when Shahid Bhai refused, saying that he was happy with his ages-old cell phone, I knew that he knew.

'Sawera, *chod apne* Shahid Bhai *ko*, you know his mood swings. Here, give this phone to me, I will keep it as part of the dowry for my daughters.' I turned my head to look amusedly at her daughters, the eldest one being barely fourteen at that time.

I told my children to get ready as we had to visit Nani-ma. I asked Fatima to come too, but she had better things to do, like have a good look at the goodies her 'little sister' had brought from Bahrain. So within the next hour or so, I was in my Ammi's arms.

As I bent down to hug this skeleton of a woman, that familiar smell of urine and sweat engulfed me – just like those days in Saudi. Only this time, my Ammi was really dying. Omar and Rashid were there too, along with Alia, my real sister and Omar's wife, all waiting for the ultimate. When I questioned my brothers as to why Ammi was not in a hospital, they told me that the doctors had given up all hope. Ammi had been suffering for a long time but holding on for probably this last meeting with her daughter.

I asked them for some space as I wanted to be left alone with this woman. This woman who took me away from my real mother. This woman who never did show any love for me. This mother who beat me up, who did not let me get educated, who called me a whore and who made me believe that perhaps I really was, because of whom today I really had become one. This woman whom I hated and whom, sadly, I still loved.

Because this woman was my mother. My only one. The one who brought me up. Why Ammi, why did you not love me . . . when you promised you would? Why did you do this to me, Ammi, why?

I needed answers, I could not let her die so easily. She looked at me and whispered, 'Sawera, my *laddo*, when I took you in my arms for the first time, I felt complete. I knew that you were all I needed but then . . . I grew greedy and started longing for a boy that Allah *miyan* graciously granted me. Not one but two. Do you know every time I beat you up for their sake, I felt more and more contempt for myself, which I never understood? I was blinded by my new love for my boys, my own flesh and blood. I did not realize that I was being unfair to you, an innocent little girl who could not even understand the changes life was bringing . . . It was only when I was abandoned by your brothers that I understood what a blunder I had committed by neglecting you all my life . . . Yes, I was and am selfish, because even when I am dying, I know that my Allah will not forgive me unless my daughter does . . . Forgive me, Sawera. I know I don't deserve it but I will not be able to die peacefully if you don't . . .'

I did. I looked straight into her sad eyes and said, 'Ammi, I forgive you.' Now, I am not one of those great souls to say that I never did have any ill feelings towards my mother, as I did. She had failed miserably in her responsibility as a mother but then probably I had, too . . . whatever the circumstances, children need their mothers the most, more than their fathers and definitely more than those clothes, toys and education that money can buy.

The whole night I was by her side, comforting her, reciting verses from the Quran and praying to Allah to make her last journey an easy one. *Jeena yahan, marna yahaan, iske sewa, jaana kahaan* . . . She listened to her last Hindi film song before the lights went off while I held her hand, before finally letting her go into the dark clouds that had enveloped the city due to the storms.

But before her last breath, she looked into my eyes pleadingly and said, 'Sawera, *meri bachchi, yeh kaam chod de,* before those flashing lights of a foreign country blind you completely, leave everything and come back.'

AUGUST 2007:

BAHRAIN

It is not that I did not listen to my dying Ammi; in fact, her death had ripped my heart apart. But I had to come back as I still had some unfinished business here. I had to make one last try to fix my life. As my visa had to be renewed and I was still hoping that Adnan Saab would let go of me and allow me to work someplace else. Maybe I could even get a new sponsor. This time, the thought of being able to call my children to Bahrain wasn't even in my mind. Over the next few days, honestly, I had lost the ability to take any more decisions, so I just let life take its course. There was a limit to how much I could plan. I was full of contradictions. So much thinking was already having an impact on me and I did not notice exactly when I fell into a phase of depression. But depression usually does not come alone; it brings with itself its friends – anxiety and insomnia. My few hours of sleep were plagued by nightmares. Every morning I would wake up in a pitiful state of extreme exhaustion.

After living like this for some time, I felt my extreme emotions turning into indifference. I had no more dreams, no complaints and no lust left in me. When Adnan Saab came to see me next, I was again ready for another important night in my life. And this time, I was going to speak the truth.

'Adnan Saab, before you come near me, I need to tell you something. I am not the same Sawera any more. All I am is a piece of meat – something that is ready to be devoured but which will not be able to respond to your touch, your kisses or your romantic overtures. All these years of being used has left me lifeless. I know that this is not what you want. I am no longer an interesting person you could have your 'communication' with or the beautiful body you lusted after. In other words, I am obsolete, completely useless for a man like you. Because even if I wanted to, I know that I will not be able to satisfy you. I just don't have it in me any more.'

While his cold eyes pierced into mine, he asked, 'What is it that you want, Sawera?'

'I want to be let free. I do not want to be paid for sex any more. I want to return to my real job – of a humble beautician. I want to still stay in Bahrain as my children need this money for their upkeep. I want to work. As I have to. But respectably. Please can you let me look for another job and transfer my visa to another sponsor if I found one?' I replied.

'Sawera, either you work for me or you go back to Pakistan. I will not let go of you as long as you are here. I don't care if you wish to be a beautician or a call girl. But I don't want Adnan Khan's mistress to be on the streets looking for work. So, for now, you can just forget about a new job or a new sponsor, as no matter what, I will not let you do it. You belong to me and no one else,' was all he said, jaws clenched, as he left the house.

That whole night I stood at the balcony watching the passers-by whose numbers kept diminishing with the breaking of dawn. I know nothing more but I woke up with the sound of the doorbell. I was still in the balcony; I had passed out when I couldn't get the answer to my question, which was if I really did love him.

Mohabbat mein nahin hai farq jeenay aur marnay ka
Usi ko dekh kar jeetay hain, jis kaafir pe dam nikle

'Oh, it's you?' was all I said and I fainted again. When I woke up, I was lying on the sofa with Rekha sitting next to my feet, massaging them gently.

I told her about my Ammi and then burst out crying. I also told her about my talk with Adnan Saab last night and sought her help. Maybe she could get me a job in her salon? Or could she help me get a free visa, though I didn't have enough money to be able to get one – but as I said, I wasn't even thinking.

It was now time for Rekha to come out with her own dirty secret.

She had been living in Bahrain for the last four-five years without even a valid visa. She belonged to a poor family in Andhra Pradesh and like the rest of her kin, she was sent here to work as a housemaid, even though she was high-school passed. Long hours, sleepless nights and excoriating work had taken a toll on her – both physically and mentally. But she carried on till she got slapped over a broken plate by her sponsor's wife. That very night she ran away from their house. In local slang, Rekha was called a 'jumping'. Instead of going to the Indian Embassy for help, she decided to carry on living here. Like all of us, she had a family back home. Poor and needy. Doing odd jobs for some time, she made friends with another beautician, who introduced her to this world. Since then, Rekha had been working in salons, but not the same one for long, out of fear of being recognized and caught. However, recently the government had declared amnesty, an opportunity for all illegal immigrants to surrender and if found clean, they would be sent to their home countries on a temporary passport or *out pass*. It was thus time for her to go home. Her husband was suffering from tuberculosis and needed her. She had made some money and could survive for another few months. And that was the farthest she could plan. She had left the reins of her life in God's hands and would go wherever her *Balaji* took her.

So that was the crux of her story. It also had an episode of 'contract marriage' but if I get into the details, it might become another book!

In other words, she was soon going to leave for good and probably would not be able to help me out. She advised me to seek help from my customers, the ones I attended to without the knowledge of Adnan Saab. I wished her luck and said goodbye to my Indian friend, just like Geetha in Saudi.

I had one such customer, whom I used to actually avoid as she gave me an unpleasant feeling when I was around her. A well-built woman from Sri Lanka, she lived in a building near mine and would call me for massage from time to time as her back hurt. But it wasn't the time to be judgemental as I needed help, from wherever it came. So when she booked me for a session in the afternoon, I did not think twice before going. And like a fool, gave up my entire story to her. Not just about my four children, which anyway my customers knew about, but that I was under the visa of a man who paid me for sex. I told her that I wanted to break away from him as I could no longer lead such a shameful life. I did not know what the solution was but I could no longer be under Adnan Saab's shadow.

After listening carefully, she gave me a lecture about women's empowerment and that I should not think of myself as a helpless, weak woman. I was strong and capable. I could do anything and be anyone I wanted. Surely she would help me get out of the muck. Completely motivated, just the way I was so many years back, in that salon with Hasan in Pakistan, I went home with newfound hope. Yes, I wasn't helpless. I was a survivor. I still had dreams. And I put my cell phone near me and waited for her call.

I jumped with joy when my cell phone rang. She told me that she had told everything about me to an acquaintance of hers, a very kind and rich man from South Africa who was in Bahrain to look for new business opportunities. He had taken pity on me and wanted to open a salon where he would employ me as the manager. It seemed he was thoroughly impressed with the account that woman had given him about my skills. She asked me to come right away as that man was in her house, waiting to interview me.

The sound of the words 'manager' and 'interview' were enough for a hopeless optimist like me to forget everything else and get ready to meet this man. I put on my black Zara trousers coupled with an off-white silk top and a string of pearls around my neck. However, I did not want to end up looking too desperate, so just chose simple flats over my favourite red stilettoes. Underplay, Sawera, just underplay.

I rehearsed some odd sentences which had the words 'clientele' and 'business expansion'. Though my grammar was not perfect, I thought I could get away with it because of this confidence I felt for the first time while facing an interview. If I could have a conversation with the super-elite in Adnan Saab's circle, then surely this so-called 'kind and rich man from South Africa' would be well . . . no big deal, as Adnan Saab would say. Yes, it wouldn't be so easy getting over such a man but for now as I stood admiring myself in the mirror, I was sure that my potential employer would not be able to reject me.

He didn't. In more ways than one. So when my Sri Lankan contact left the house so that we could discuss things in peace, I still could not fathom that I was making the same mistake. Again. And this time this South African facing me wasn't in any way Adnan Saab. He was going to get what he bargained for. At all costs.

After the expected questions about my background and experience, the fat bastard rose up from the sofa as if he had had enough. He came towards me and moved closer to kiss me. Before I could react, he punched my face before pushing me down on the floor and laid his entire body on me, while moving his hands frantically over my shirt to unbutton it. As I lay there, suffocated with shock and fear, all I could do was count the pearls from my broken necklace, scattered all over the ground.

I don't how long I lay there frozen and stunned, in pain, and staring at the ceiling above my head. When I came to my senses there was no sign of my rapist or his procuress. I was all alone. In a strange house. All fucked up. Literally.

I rose up from the floor and went to the bathroom. Just the way they show in films, as I had no idea what else I was supposed to do. Even as the hot water dripped over my body, I felt so numb and dazed that for a moment I wasn't even sure if this was really happening. Probably I had fallen asleep on the balcony again and it had rained. But then I looked around this bathroom, studying the unfamiliar bottles of shampoo and body lotions, and looked at my wet body, my wet hair and felt my wet eyes. No, it wasn't a dream. It had happened to me. I got raped. By a man who was supposed to be an answer to all my problems. I felt extreme nausea and exhaustion. I vomited and was tempted to pass out. I closed my eyes to stop the ground spinning beneath my feet. But who would look after me in this house? What if the man came back? Where should I go? Who would believe a prostitute who claimed to have been raped? Why did I come here? What did I want, anyway? I was confused, guilty and was having a breakdown. But a part of my mind was still alert and in control. Put on your clothes and get out of here, Sawera. Just get out.

As I staggered out of the building, like a drunken loose woman, I felt mortified. Everyone was staring. They were all mocking me. Look at this whore, she deserved it, that bitch. I heard these voices calling me names, laughing away. The voices belonged to Ammi and then I heard Fatima laughing the loudest.

I almost tripped on a stone of the pavement before I felt hands gripping my arms. 'Madam, what happened? You look sick . . . come, I will take you home.' As I tried recognizing him, I felt his hand brush against my chest. Even though I knew it wasn't deliberate and the poor delivery guy from my diet food company was just trying to help, I shouted at him: '*Kameene*, you want to touch me? You want to feel me? You want to fuck me? You dog, all you men are the same . . . come, I will give it you!' I cried while tearing my blouse apart, giving the bewildered passers-by a good look at my bust. I still cannot forget the expression on the Bangladeshi's face as he saw this crazy woman in a red bra, shouting and screaming at him in the middle of the road. What could he do except flee from the scene?

Thankfully, my building wasn't that far from there and I somehow managed to reach it. The watchman brought me up and closed the door behind me before calling up Adnan Saab.

Since I was safe, I could now afford to pass out.

When I woke up, I saw Adnan Saab sitting on the sofa opposite, reading a newspaper. 'Sawera, are you all right? Do you want tea?'

I got up from the sofa and fell down at his feet. 'Adnan Saab, he raped me, do you know, he raped me, that bastard . . .' I told him everything.

'That is why, Sawera, I told you to not go out looking for work,' he said softly. I wasn't the only one who had lost something. He had, too.

'You need to get a grip on things, Sawera. What happened to you was barbaric, inhuman and unfortunate, to say the least. But I promise you that they will be punished, I will make sure they spend the rest of their lives behind bars. You will not be involved in this mess again; I have my contacts who will do it for me. But you will make a promise to me to that you will recover. And this time, you have all the time in the world to heal your body and your mind. Your children will be sent money, don't worry about that, and I will not touch you ever again. Not because I consider you dirty but because your days of living this life are over. Once you are ready, tell me and I will send you back. But in the meantime, you will do as I say. Tomorrow you have an appointment with a friend of mine, a leading psychologist who will help you deal with this trauma. Not only that, she will help you deal with everything else that has happened in your life. Cooperate with her. And help her to help you. As I said, take your time.' Adnan Saab's voice was authoritative, yet gentle.

'Why, Adnan Saab, why are you doing this for me?' I asked.

'I am not doing it for you, Sawera,' was all he said as he closed the door behind him, disappearing from my life.

Ya Khuda, so Adnan Saab was my *farishta*. Yes, despite what happened between us, he became someone I would always look up to. As for the first time in my life, I had a man like him taking complete charge of my life. A man I surrendered to, willingly. In body and now in soul. And I remembered Hasan's words when he said, '*He is an honourable, well-respected person. All right, he has had some random girlfriends but nobody is perfect, all he wants is some love. Surely you could do that much for him?*'

While I had started to love him, it was now time to do something for myself. Adnan Saab's orders.

For the next two months or so, all I did was pray. I stopped calling up my family in Pakistan, I stopped all those beauty treatments and diet food. I started buying my own groceries and cooking my own *dal-chawal*. I would say my *Namaz* five times a day but prayed almost all the time. It was time for *tawbah* (repentance). It was time for *Al-Ghafur, Al-Afuww*, (the Forgiving, the Pardoner) to forgive me for my sins.

And it was also time to go visit the Grand Mosque I had been attracted by when I came to Bahrain the first time. This magnificent structure, which can hold thousands of worshippers, was built with marble from Italy, glass from Austria and teak from India. Bahraini craftsmen had carved it into a fine example of interior design. Henceforth, like an eager tourist, every day I visited at least one famous place. I wanted to make the most of my limited days in Bahrain. I discovered all the treasures of this little island – its National Museum, the Souk, Zallaq beach, the forts. Almost everything. A visit to the 'Tree of Life' – a natural wonder, standing tall and alone in the heart of the desert for hundreds of years, without any water supply, gave me my inspiration to survive. I also discovered another amazing aspect. This

Muslim country has a number of temples, churches and gurudwaras, and people, including expatriates, are free to practise their own religion and celebrate all festivals together. If only the whole world became as accepting and tolerant . . .

My sessions with the psychologist were helping too. Slowly I was coming out of my shell and was able to express the deep-rooted anger in myself. I opened the wounds of the past all over again and talked about everything that had happened to me, good and bad, that made me the person I was.

She told me that anger is energizing whereas depression is the opposite: it is anger turned inwards. Yes, I was allowed to be angry – at my regrettable life, my dead self-centred Ammi, my children who were shackles gripping my feet, my ex-husbands, my ex-sponsor in Saudi, Adnan Saab and even all those women out there who did not have to struggle like me, who were born into loving families, who had husbands who took charge of everything while they stayed at home, looking after their children. Yes, I was really, really angry at those 'average' housewives who have no idea how lucky they are. I laughed, I cried, I banged my head, I beat my chest and I finally learnt to let go.

I learnt to give in, too. Because I realized that no matter how much I tried to force a result, a future that I had dreamt of, ultimately everything was in my God's hands. For the first time in my life, I did not have a plan. All I had to do was my best and live in the present. And trust HIM. And once I started believing in this, unconditionally – everything became all right.

When the call from Pakistan came again, I realized it was time to head home.

PRESENT DAY:

BAHRAIN

'**S**o that's about it, madam, the story of my life – a classic example of '*nau sou chuhe khake billi Haj ko chali,*' she concluded, laughing, with the last stroke of her magical fingers on my pampered back.

I rose with a jerk. 'Oh no, Sawera, this is not the story of your life, I mean it is, but you haven't told me *everything*. What was that call about? What happened after you went to Pakistan? How did you come back to Bahrain and when? Where are your children?' I begged. Surely she couldn't just leave me wanting more, like this?

By now, she seemed rather exhausted. Though I knew I was being a bitch by probing her to go on, I had to know everything.

'Sawera, I deserve to know. I mean you said you will do anything for me, right? You don't have to get into the details but please, please answer my questions,' I requested.

'Madam, maybe it is not so interesting any more. I mean, it is no big deal,' said she, perhaps thinking of the same man again who taught her to use phrases like this.

'OK, Sawera, let's go slow. I won't push you. What was that call about? Secondly, you don't have to call me madam. You know my name and you are the owner of a successful business, after all,' said I, confident that now she would go on.

'The call was from Rashid,' she said.

'Apparently, in her *wasiyatnama*, Ammi had declared my brothers and me as equal beneficiaries of her property, basically that old house that Abbu built from his life's savings. The house was old and not maintained but it happened to be in a 'decent locality' so it had 'good market value'. She had instructed them to dispose of it and buy separate houses for each of us from the sales proceeds. They were able to sell the house and had identified a small flat for me, which they could finalize if I said yes, or I could even keep my share.

'A homeless woman like me knew what it meant to have a roof over my head, a place to keep my children. I did not think twice before asking Rashid to buy that flat. Moreover, it was what Ammi wanted,' Sawera narrated.

'Oh, so now that you had a house, you could go back, right? Did you really trust your brothers to not dupe you into this deal? Why didn't they tell you before? Did you even have a good look at the *wasiyat*?' I enquired.

'Oh, it's not what you are thinking. They did not call up as they wanted to be sure about finalizing the flat for me. And Ammi was a very wise woman, she had nominated, rather requested, Shahid Bhai, Fatima's honest, no-nonsense husband, to look after her vulnerable daughter's interests and make sure there was no hanky-panky in these transactions,' Sawera replied.

'Hanky-panky . . . Adnan's words again . . . what about him, Sawera? Wait – first tell me what happened in Pakistan?' I questioned.

'Nothing much, except that I got married again,' Sawera answered.

'Shut up!! You got married again? And you say it's no big deal?' I exclaimed. 'Sawera, I am not going to let you go now, I don't care how tired you are.'

When she realized that I was a woman on a mission, she gave in.

'**M**a'am, please can you help? I think I am not able to get a good grip on this thread.' This girl with a *hijab* framing her oval face and with the tiniest adult body I had ever seen, asked me, embarrassed.

'Here, let me show you how. What did I tell you, take a while to think . . . plan, OK?' I outlined the eyebrows of this other girl with a pencil. Then I took a lash comb and swept the hair up and then down to trim the number of tiny hairs that were standing out. Finally, I made a large loop by tying the two ends of the thread, and then twisted the thread at the middle a few times.

'Make sure you apply some powder. Now see the movements of my hands: open – close, open – close, open – close the loops while keeping the twisted part on the unwanted hair,' I instructed while working on those bushy eyebrows, leaving the victim with tears in her eyes. But both girls looked really pleased at the end result – a beautiful smooth black arch over that red eye – and thanked me.

As I turned around in the direction of the usual sounds of giggling from a group of girls who were trying their hand at makeup, perhaps for the first time in their lives, I looked up to thank Allah again. For this day.

I was now working as an instructor in a vocational training institute for women, an NGO near my new house. The place was not 'happening', the girls mostly from poor families and the money not great, but I was at peace with myself.

It was a chance encounter with Iqbal, the youngest brother of my first husband, that had really turned the tide. It had been about three or four months since my return to Pakistan. I had finished whatever little money I had and was looking for a job. My children and I were no longer living with Fatima. I had my own little cocoon, a one-bedroom flat in a new colony on the outskirts of the city. With a school nearby, a community park and a small grocery store, it was paradise. It had to be, my angels were with me. It was now time to complete those stories of little fairies who lived in palaces made of chocolates and who spent all their time in playing, chasing butterflies and dancing in magnificent gardens full of red roses. The fairies were even happier since their mother had come back after fighting the demons, far, far away. Life was simple, sometimes boring, but we were happy. And together. Except that I wasn't left with much money. But I was sure something would work out. And it did.

It wasn't a very happy time in Adil Chacha's house, though. The poor man had died of extreme neglect from his three sons and their wives, who lived in the same house. It was the same old story of large families having to share a small space. Coupled with materialism and lack of resources. Same story. Different house.

Iqbal, however lived separately since he had left that house, all those years back. He was now involved in social causes and worked for 'women's right to live without violence'. I met him when I had visited Adil Chacha's house to express my condolences. We spoke about *marhoom* Chacha's love for *noon chai*, nihaari and mutton korma. I couldn't help still being amused at the fact that even if they had never had a lot of money, they had invested well in food. Those were the days, back then I was so young and so restless. When I asked Iqbal about his family, he told me that he had none. Iqbal had not married. And Wasim – that unlucky bastard did not or could not have children from his second wife. The other two brothers had three wives and five children between them, who quarrelled with each other all the time.

I left, relieved that Wasim was not home or it would have been really awkward to face him – the father of my children, the first man to have used and abused me. I did not know, however, that it wasn't the end of my association with this house.

To cut a long story short, it was Iqbal who helped me get this job. And it was Iqbal whom I married.

BAHRAIN AGAIN –

PRESENT DAY

'**W**hat? You married Iqbal, your youngest brother-in-law? You are joking, right?' I couldn't stop laughing.

'I did. Rather he made me. As even when I said 'yes' to him, I wasn't sure if I was doing the right thing. It all began when I started my work with this NGO that he had some contacts in. He used to visit the place regularly to get updates on the progress of our training programmes. Some of my students were referred to us by his organization that worked for the safety of women against domestic violence and acid attacks. The victims were encouraged to get out of their society-imposed boundaries and stand up for themselves. For me it was an extremely fascinating and rewarding experience. When I met women who had gone through the most brutal and savage of physical and mental torture, I forgot about my own miseries of the past. I became more and more involved in finding a better future for these unfortunate girls.

'I also learnt to forgive my family. Fatima and I actually became as sisters should be, now that there wasn't the baggage of my children or my money between us. Even Omar and Rashid got closer to me, and to each other, especially now that Ammi was no more. Rashid told me that Ammi really was worried about me and remembered me all the time in her last days. Yes, she did love me.

'Iqbal had a major influence on me those days and he still has. He motivated me to move on and complete my education. He used to visit my house a lot and would play with my children, who loved him like their own. He was my 'friend, philosopher and guide', just the way you Indians say. I had told him everything about my past, including my relationship with Adnan Saab. But he said it did not matter to him as it was our future together that counted. He admitted to having had feelings for me since the time I was still his brother's wife.

'I did not want to get married at all as I thought I could finally take care of myself and my children and honestly did not feel the need of a man. He told me that it was he who needed me and even now, when I was an independent woman, I should give love a chance. It wasn't so easy convincing me to marry him, as after going through that hell, I thought I had lost the capacity to love again. But as I said before, love always finds a way. And time is the biggest healer. So after about a year of him pursuing me, I said yes. It has now been seven years, *Alhamdulillah.*'

'Wow . . . so how and when did you guys come to Bahrain?' I was getting impatient now.

'It was a few years back. I was pregnant again, when one day Iqbal came home from work, all excited. He had applied for a job with another NGO and, by the grace of God, received his appointment letter. A job with a better position and more money. But it was in another city. Actually, another country. Of course, you know which one.' She smiled.

She continued, 'So we came here, this time absolutely legally on a family visa. Along with our five children. Finally, I was able to fulfil the promise I made to them years ago. When my youngest one started kindergarten, I knew it was now time to take care of that 'unfinished business' I had left in Bahrain. I was now a qualified, respectable professional and within a few months, found a local partner who invested in this salon: Reshma Salon and Spa.'

'Oh . . . my congratulations, Sawera; so everything worked out for you. I am so happy to know your children are here with you,' I said.

'Oh yes, you will be happier to know that they all go to one of the most prestigious schools of the country. My daughters are big now . . . and smart too . . . Sana will be joining medical college next year and Suhana wants to get into the 'beauty' business, just like her mother. But Naveed and Aftab, you know, they are just boys and refuse to grow up. Average, rebellious teens always on Facebook-shacebook! But I am sure they will eventually follow their sisters' lead. Of course, having Iqbal as a role model will help. So I am not worried,' she said confidently, impressing me again with her positivity and hope for the future.

'Oh, that's wonderful, Sawera, but what about your husband in Saudi, what was his name again – Hamid? And that lady, your sponsor? Were you able to take your revenge?' I probed – probably the wrong questions – as I waited anxiously for her to speak...

'I am nobody to punish anyone . . . it is Allah who will take an account from them . . . honestly, I don't even care enough to find out. I have mellowed down, you see, and I don't want to lose my sleep over these trivial things. I have a business to run, after all . . . And I really think it's time to call it a day.' She sighed, looking at her watch, all set to go.

'One last question.' I stood up, blocking her way. 'What about Adnan? I am sorry to remind you, but you said you loved him . . . Are you not in touch with him?' I brought up yet another touchy topic.

'Adnan Saab . . . yes, I did love him. We are not in touch at all. I have moved on and so has he. But you will not believe it, I met him by chance, a few months back in Dubai where he now lives. He was with this beautiful mature woman in an elegant *salwar kameez*. He looked content and proudly introduced her as his wife. His third one, I guess. And this time, an actual college professor, no less. So he finally got what he really wanted.' She laughed, genuinely happy.

'And so did you, Sawera. *Bhagwaan ka shukar hai*,' I said, as I picked up my bag to leave the salon.

AFTERWORD

SOME YEARS AGO: 'THAT' NIGHT IN BAHRAIN

'You need to get a grip on things, Sawera. What happened to you was barbaric, inhuman and unfortunate, to say the least. But I promise you that they will be punished, I will make sure they spend the rest of their lives behind bars. You will not be involved in this mess again; I have my contacts who will do it for me. But you will make a promise to me to that you will recover. And this time, you have all the time in the world to heal your body and your mind. Your children will be sent money, don't worry about that, and I will not touch you ever again. Not because I consider you dirty but because your days of living this life are over. Once you are ready, tell me and I will send you back. But in the meantime, you will do as I say. Tomorrow you have an appointment with a friend of mine, a leading psychologist who will help you deal with this trauma. Not only that, she will help you deal with everything else that has happened in your life. Cooperate with her. And help her to help you. As I said, take your time.' Adnan's voice was authoritative, yet gentle.

'Why, Adnan Saab, why are you doing this for me?' Sawera asked

'I am not doing it for you, Sawera,' was all he said when he closed the door behind him, disappearing from her life.

As his driver parked the Lexus in the garage of Adnan's palatial bungalow in one of the most posh compounds in Bahrain, he noticed his 'Sir' looked more disturbed than he had ever seen him. Something was really wrong, but then he was just a driver, so what could he do anyway, he thought.

Adnan went up to his study and made some calls. Some calls about the rape of a woman he knew closely. That he wanted those criminals to pay for it. And pay heavily.

And then he made another call. A call to Pakistan.

'Yes, Rashid, I know everything. So please don't bother. Just listen carefully. Your sister is in pain. She has no one to look after her, despite having you all. She doesn't deserve it and you need to do as I say. You will call her to say that your Ammi has left a third of her property to Sawera . . . yes, you heard it right . . . with that money you will buy a small flat for her. Not lavish, as we want it to seem believable. If you want to involve others in the family too, I don't mind, but make it happen. I don't want Sawera to be at anyone's mercy when she is back. You will all support her and make her feel at home. In return you will get paid, and paid well . . . yes, you will . . . you should. I will tell you exactly when to call her up, right now she is recovering. But you have to promise that no matter what happens, you will never, never ever let her know about our deal.'

'But, Adnan Saab, why are you doing this for Sawera?' Rashid asked.

'That, my friend, is none of your business,' was all Adnan said as he put down the phone.

A NOTE FROM THE AUTHOR

Dear Readers,

If you have read so far or even if you haven't, I would still like to thank you for being interested in reading this note from me. It is not part of the story but I really feel I owe some clarifications to everyone.

Firstly, though the story is fictitious, it is loosely based on some real-life events but is not any one particular woman's narrative. Over the last few years, I have come across a few women who have left their homes to work abroad to fund a secure future for their children. I have utmost respect for them, as well as for the central character in my story, who has to fulfil her responsibilities by working as a 'mistress'. I sincerely feel that whatever women do, wherever they do it, out of choice or not, to provide for their families – is honest and honourable work.

Secondly, the story is not about life in the Gulf. The word 'bahir' means outside in Urdu and in some Indian languages too, which is used as a metaphor for 'abroad'. Here is a restless soul who wants to go out and expects solutions for a better life from a land different than her own. But they say the grass is greener on the other side only when it is fake. Coming back to the point, the story is set against the backdrops of Saudi Arabia and

Bahrain but it is not about these countries. I have lived in the beautiful country of Bahrain for a long time but still do not claim to be fully aware of everything about it. This is a work of imagination and should be treated as such. I might have taken some liberties in explaining some events or places but my intention is not at all to judge, be it a country or its people. Also, just for the sake of simplicity, I have not gone into the particulars of the legal paperwork needed to work, get married or divorced in these countries, either. The story could happen anywhere – in America, Australia or Japan. The central character could be from anywhere, too. I have just watched a lot of Pakistani TV serials and find their women interesting and that is the only reason for creating 'Sawera'. Even the other 'shady' characters, of a Sri Lankan or a South African, are not intentional – you could replace them with natives of any other country yet the meaning or outcome will remain the same.

Thirdly, I have utmost regard for all religions and communities. While this 'disclaimer' gets mentioned before the story starts, I would again like to emphasize the fact that I have absolutely no intention of offending the sentiments of any religion or community, or even country, for that matter, as being a proud Indian, I truly believe in the concept of *Vasudhaiva Kutumbakam*.

Finally, I hope you will read the book with an open mind and an open heart for a woman who struggles all her life to give herself and her children a feeling of being wanted and who thought that money would do it for her. And I hope that, like her, we all realize that it is love which is the most valuable gift from the universe. The lack of it can destroy a soul. And a life full of it is the only life worth living. Yes, you have heard this before but a little reminder never hurt anyone, did it?

God bless and peace to all . . .
Monisha

GLOSSARY

Aakhri nishaani	Last keepsake/reminder
Aalu gosht.	Dish made of potatoes (aalu) and meat (gosht)
Aaya	Maid/nanny
Abaya	Cloak/full-dress, mostly black
Abbu	Father
Alhamdulillah	In praise of God/Thank God
Allah meherban to gadha pehelwan	Literal meaning: If God is generous than even a donkey can be a wrestler. In other words, all you need is God's kindness to succeed.
Al-Muhaymin	God the Guardian
Amanat	A thing precious to its owner, given to a loyal person to keep it safe
Ammi	Mother
Angrez	Englishman
Apa	Elder sister
Appams	South Indian pancakes
Arbab	Sponsor of visa / employer in Gulf countries
Ar-Rahman, Ar-Rahim	The Most Gracious, The Most Merciful
Asmaan se gira, khajoor main atka	Literally, fell from the sky and got stuck in a date palm. To come out from one trouble but get caught in another

Badshaguni	Evil/curse
Bahir	Outside but typically used to mean 'foreign country'
Baklava	Rich, sweet dessert pastry
Bazaaru aurat	Prostitute
Bhabhi	Sister-in-law (brother's wife)
Bhai	Brother
Bhagwaan ka shukar hai	Thank God in Hindi
Chacha	Father's brother; uncle
Chachi	Uncle's wife
Chai-Patti	Tea leaves
Chod apne Shahid Bhai ko	Leave your brother Shahid alone
Dadi	Grandmother (father's mother)
Dai-ma	Midwife
Dal	Lentils
Dal-chawal	Lentil soup/curry with rice
Desi ghee	Clarified butter
Djinns	Ghosts/spirits
Do number ki aurat	Dishonourable woman
Dupatta	A long piece of cloth worn around the head, neck and shoulders by women
Farishta	A guardian angel
Faux pas	Blunder
Ganwaar	Uneducated
Gosht	Mutton
Gurbat	Poverty/helplessness
Halwa-puri	A popular dish in Pakistan/North India, of a sweet semolina preparation (halwa) with deep-fried unleavened flatbreads (puri)

Haram	Forbidden (typically in Islam)
Haramzadi	Cuss-word meaning despicable female. Literally, female born of unwed parents
Hijab	Head-scarf
Hunar	Skill/talent
Ikama	Identity/residency card
Jahannum	Hell
Jahil	Illiterate
Jalebia	Dress worn mostly by Arab women
Jawan hatte-katte	Young, well-built
Jeena yahan, marna yahaan, iske sewa, jaana kahaan	Old Bollywood song. The lyrics mean 'Here we live, here we die, Other than here, where would we go'
Jugadu	Street-smart/resourceful
Jutties	Shoes
Kahwa	Traditional tea preparation
Kameene	Cuss-word meaning rascal, despicable one
Keema parathas	Fried flatbread stuffed with minced meat
Khairiyat?	All OK?
Khala	Mother's sister
Khalu	Uncle (mother's sister's husband)
Korma	A rich meat curry with a bit of thick sauce
Kurta	Garment resembling a shirt, usually without a collar
La-la-la-la lori, doodh ki katori . .	Urdu/Hindi lullaby
Lazeez	Delicious
Lehenga	Long exquisite skirt
Lungi	Sarong-like garment wrapped round the waist
Ma-behen ki gaaliyan	Cuss words involving mother and sister

Madrasa	Islamic school
Mamools	Small Lebanese shortbread pastries stuffed with dates or nuts
Manhoos	Cursed/unlucky
Marhoom	Dead
Masha-Allah	As Allah wills; uttered in thankfulness (usually to ward off the evil eye)
Masoom	Innocent
Mehendi laga ke rakhna, doli saja ke rakhna	Famous Bollywood song typically played during wedding celebrations by Indians/Pakistanis. Meaning, 'Decorate yourself with henna, keep the (wedding) palanquin decorated and ready'
Meri bachchi, yeh kaam chod de	My daughter, let go of this job/work
Miyan	Respectful address by a male to another male
Mohalla	Area/compound
Mubarak	Congratulations
Naan	A flat leavened white bread
Nashta	Breakfast
Nau sou chuhe khake billi Haj ko chali	Literal meaning: After eating 900 rates, the cat went off on a Haj (a pious visit to Mecca). In other words, after being 'bad' and doing wrong for a long time, now treading a righteous path
Nihaari	Rich meat stew
Nikah	Wedding
Paan	Betel leaves
Pagal ho gayee hai kya?	Have you gone mad?
Pathani suit	Dress worn by men from the Northwest Frontier region

Pir baba	Spiritual guide/saint
Pranayama	A series of breathing exercises practised in Yoga
Qabul Hai	Accepted
Qayamat	Doomsday (End of the world)
Qazi	Authoritative man/guide who can perform certain rituals in Islam
Rakhael	Prostitute, kept woman
Ramzaan/Ramadan	Holy month of fasting for Muslims
Randi	Prostitute/slut
Rasm-e-henna	Wedding custom of decorating hands with intricate designs using henna (the paste of henna leaves acts as a dye)
Rogan josh	Meat dish
Sabzi	Vegetables
Salwar	A pair of loose trousers
Sambar	Spicy South-Indian curry dish of lentils and vegetables
Sangeet	Music (Ladies' Sangeet: Musical night, typically during wedding celebrations)
Sarparast	Protector/In-charge
Sasur	Father-in-law
Sau sunhaar ki, ek louhaar ki	A hundred blows from goldsmith are matched by one blow from an ironsmith
Sawera (name of protagonist)	Morning
Seekh-kebab	Skewered and grilled spicy minced meat/chicken
Shaayeri	Urdu poetry
Sharara	Traditional trousers, gathered at the hips and flowing loosely down to the feet, teamed with a long shirt, worn by Muslim ladies

Shareef, khandaani	Decent, from a good family
Shohar	Husband
Suhaag raat	Wedding night
Talaq	Divorce
Talaqshuda	Divorcée
Tayajaan	Uncle (father's elder brother)
Thobe	Long garment, mostly white or grey, worn by Arab males
Unparh	Uneducated
Utha le mujhe	Lift me up (addressed to God, meaning, I want to die)
Wasiyatnama	Last will and testament (official papers/decree)
Ya Khuda!	Oh God!
Zillat	Dishonour

MEANING OF THE VERSES BY THE GREAT AND FAMOUS POET MIRZA GHALIB

Hazaaron khwahishen aisi ke har khwahish pe dam nikle, *Bohat niklay mere armaan, lekin phir bhi kam nikle*	Having thousands of desires, all worth dying for Many desires were fulfilled, but still not enough
Nikalna khuld se aadam ka sunte aaye the lekin, *Bade be-aabru hokar tere kooche se hum nikley . . .*	We have been hearing of Adam's dismissal from Heaven, Completely humiliated, I am walking out from your streets
Mohabbat mein nahin hai farq jeenay aur marnay ka *Usi ko dekh kar jeetay hain, jis kaafir pe dam nikle*	When in love, there is no difference between being alive or dead I live just looking at the non-believer/infidel for whom I would die

CPSIA information can be obtained
at www.ICGtesting.com
Printed in the USA
LVHW111044161118
597074LV00003B/35/P